JUAN EMAR

*TRANSLATED FROM THE SPANISH
BY MEGAN McDOWELL*

Peirene

Ayer

TRANSLATOR

Megan McDowell has translated many of the most important Latin American writers working today, including Mariana Enríquez, Lina Meruane, Samanta Schweblin and Alejandro Zambra. Her translations have won the English PEN Award and the Premio Valle Inclán, and have been nominated three times for the International Booker Prize. Her short-story translations have appeared in the *New Yorker*, the *Paris Review* and *Granta*, among others. In 2020 she won an Award in Literature from the American Academy of Arts and Letters. She is from Richmond, Kentucky, and lives in Santiago, Chile.

Peirene

JUAN EMAR

TRANSLATED FROM THE SPANISH
BY MEGAN McDOWELL

Yesterday

First published in Great Britain in 2021 by
Peirene Press Ltd
17 Cheverton Road
London N19 3BB
www.peirenepress.com

First published in 1935 under the original Spanish-language title *Ayer* by Juan Emar
© 1935, Juan Emar
© 2019, by Fundación Juan Emar

This translation of Ayer is published by arrangement with the Ampi Margini literary
agency and with the authorization of the Fundación Juan Emar

English-language translation copyright © 2021, Megan McDowell
Introduction copyright © 2021, Alejandro Zambra

ISBN 978-1-908670-65-6

Designed by Sacha Davison Lunt
Cover illustration by Caroline McArthur
Typeset by Tetragon, London
Printed and bound by TJ Books, Padstow, Cornwall

CONTENTS

INTRODUCTION

Juan Emar's Olympic Games

In a diary entry from his youth, Juan Emar writes that if he had been born in ancient Greece, he would have dedicated his life entirely to art, in a perpetual and delicious solitude interrupted only by 'the obnoxious Olympic Games'. It seems that, from a very early age, Emar fantasized about a life dedicated to creation. Still, he didn't want to 'be a writer', much less to behave like one. He wanted to write, to give himself over to pure leisure, to the search, fearlessly tuning in to mystery and uncertainty. And this life dedicated to art and introspection is the one that we can intuit for the narrator of *Yesterday*, who wanders about the fictional city of San Agustín de Tango (Emar's Macondo or Yoknapatawpha, which in any case would sound familiar to a Chilean ear: <u>San</u> Agus<u>tín</u> de T<u>ango</u>) searching for a 'conclusion' or illumination that remains always just out of reach. His wanderings, however, take place not in solitude, but in the company of his wife and a rotating cast of characters, including a painter whose love for the colour green is as deep-seated as his hatred for the bourgeoisie; a pot-bellied man who is a stand-in for every story under the sun; a poor soul whose generosity gets him beheaded; plus the narrator's family and the Uruguayan consul.

Juan Emar (1893–1964) was born Álvaro Yáñez Bianchi but was 'Pilo' to his friends, and later, during his years as an art critic, he went by the name Jean Emar: 'J'en ai marre', which means 'I'm fed up' in French. Indeed, he was a contemporary not of Pindar but of André Breton, and he wasn't born in the country of Homer but rather that of Vicente Huidobro and Pablo Neruda, to name two poets who were enemies of each other but friends to Emar. Especially Huidobro, to whom, nevertheless, the following phrase is attributed, about as friendly as a knife in the back: 'Pilo writes with his feet.' Neruda, on the other hand, wrote a generous prologue in 1971, well after Emar's death, that began like this: 'I knew Juan Emar intimately without ever knowing him. He had great friends who were never his friends.'

Emar published little and late and strangely. In June 1935, at the age of forty-one, he self-published three brilliant novels en bloc: *Miltín 1934*, *Un año* (*One Year*) and, perhaps the best of them, *Ayer* (*Yesterday*). Then, in 1937, the Editorial Universitaria published *Diez* (*Ten*), which I consider one of the best story collections of Spanish-language literature, though I say that from the future, of course; in Emar's present, the book found few readers. It failed in much the same way as his novels, which were absolute critical and popular flops. Today it seems a mystery how a millionaire aristocrat, whose father founded a newspaper and was president of the Senate of Chile, could fail so spectacularly. One obvious but insufficient explanation is his staunch, dogged avant-gardism, and surely his aversion to literary critics didn't help, leading him to include in his novel *Miltín 1934*, for example, a direct attack on the very critic who could have helped to improve his public standing, Alone (that was the absurd pseudonym used by Hernán Díaz Arrieta: Alone, the greatest taste-maker in Chilean literature, later humorously fictionalized by Roberto Bolaño with the name Farewell). His contempt for critics was legendary ('I don't want to hear comments from critics and more critics, I don't want to learn the opinions of beings who turn what they read into a profession to earn a living') and also extended to the art world. In fact, he would often lay into other critics in his own art reviews (I remember one very funny piece in which he cites the example of a critic who was despondent because he couldn't figure out whether the fruits he'd seen in a still-life painting were apples or plums).

Perhaps the books he published in his lifetime were Emar's Olympic Games. Because after those he swore never to compete again, to publish nothing more, and in fact he transformed non-publication into a kind of personal mission ('My refuge consisted in not publishing, no, never publishing again, until others whom I didn't know would publish me while they sat on the steps of my tomb'). As I have already said, he didn't want to be a writer but to write, and that's precisely what he did during the last twenty years of his life, which he dedicated entirely to his massive project *Umbral* (*Threshold*).

'I'm still writing every day,' Emar says in a letter in 1959. 'I'm on page 3,332. When this is published it'll make for an immense number of volumes. When? After I die!!' The manuscript eventually swelled to over five thousand pages, the first volume appearing in Argentina in 1971, published by Carlos Lohlé. Then, in 1996, thirty-two years after his death, Emar's monumental work was finally published in its entirety, in five volumes that totalled 4,135 cramped pages (in a normal-sized font it could easily have reached six or seven thousand).

This is not, however, a Hollywood biopic, or even a Netflix series... And then again, maybe it is. But it's not over yet, we're only halfway through, say at the end of the first season. Even today it's almost absurd to present Emar as a *forgotten* writer, since he has never been, so to speak, sufficiently remembered. In spite of a few tons of doctoral theses and improved access to digital versions of his books (the Chilean National Library has uploaded almost all his works in some foggy but free PDFs), Emar is still far from occupying the place he deserves in Chilean literature. The matter becomes even more critical if we broaden our scope beyond national borders, since although there have been publications in Argentina and Spain, his work is still a fundamentally Chilean phenomenon or epiphenomenon. As for other languages, so far he has been translated only into French and Portuguese; this is his first book in English (although the *Review of Contemporary Fiction* did dedicate a special issue to him in 2007 with translations by Daniel Borzutzky). This implies an additional layer of irony, because there are few writers in Chile who had such an international background as Emar, who knew, for example, the twentieth-century French avant-garde like the back of his hand, and first-hand at that. Maybe Emar's scarcity in English translation has to do with the fact that he doesn't fit the Anglophone idea of a Latin American author, having more in common with European surrealist writers, or Fauvist or Dadaist artists. I have the feeling that English-language readers are willing now to rescue him from the literary seclusion to which he was relegated by his anachronistic internationalism.

Nevertheless, there are many of us now who grew up reading and admiring him. I was fourteen years old when I first read 'El pájaro verde' ('The Green Bird'), his most famous story, and I couldn't stop laughing, but it was only in college that I read him seriously and fell in love with him. Though maybe I should talk about polyamory, because there were six or seven of us who loved Juan Emar and had the unexpected pleasure of discovering him together, every Friday, in the long and intense classes given by a specialist in his work who was only a little less young than we were, and who loved Emar with a sweeping and perfectly reasoned madness. Emar's avant-gardism was, of course, old-fashioned, *traditional*, and that's how we read him in part, though his fidelity to avant-garde procedures, tricks and slogans didn't explain our love for his work then and doesn't explain it now. His writing didn't sound old to us, it sounded furious and prematurely contemporary, as perhaps Emar himself expected or presupposed, if one can judge from his constant and bitter reflections about posterity and literary fame, which were present, for example, in *Miltín 1934* ('Why give such importance to gentlemen from the year 2000 and onward? What if they turn out to be a pack of cretins?'). I suppose that these days we've grown more used to the incursion of unreality in art, and we feel less shocked by – to borrow Lautréamont's lovely description of beauty so often quoted by surrealists – 'the chance meeting on a dissecting-table of a sewing-machine and an umbrella'. Emar's experimentation with form would have been more shocking in his day, a direct refutation of the serious and often boring realism that was the more establishment, *criollismo* of contemporary prose writers. Today we focus on other things: the first pages of this novel, for example, appear to a Chilean reader as a direct indictment of our country's conservatism, which unfortunately we still know so well. But it is perhaps his indescribable sense of humour that most attracted us to Emar, a perfectly recognizable humour, though as with all truly good humorists, we often don't know whether his narrators are speaking seriously or in jest. In this sense, Emar is to prose what Nicanor Parra is to Chilean poetry, and maybe the combination of their influences can explain many particularities of our so often anti-literary Chilean literature.

In his 1971 prologue to *Diez*, Neruda pretty haphazardly compares Emar to Kafka, thus generating an instant blurb that is a little unfair, because Emar was not the Chilean Kafka, just as Neruda himself wasn't the Chilean Whitman. Chileans my age were lucky enough to read Emar without needing to apply that kind of comparison, though I do understand the impulse. I remember we spent one class arguing over whether Emar was superior to Cortázar, who at the time, in the mid-1990s, was unanimously considered to be the paradigm of the super-writer, valued in equal measure by aesthetes, essentialists, vitalists and speculators. We never reached a conclusion, but I remember that someone – it wasn't the professor, who was unusually reserved that day, limiting himself to semi-silently savouring his victory because in a matter of weeks he had managed to turn us into Juan Emar fanatics – proclaimed that in the future no one would read Cortázar any more, and in that future Emar's work would be at the centre of the canon, and we were all more or less in agreement. It was a reckless and clearly nationalist idea, and a stupid one, because why did we even need to force a competition between two writers we adored? But it was the 1990s, a horrible time when at least we could give ourselves the luxury of pretending to be Harold Bloom during discussions that tended to end in explosions of lysergic laughter.

Juan Emar, ahead of his time, was no doubt writing for readers of the future, and it's as arrogant as it is exciting to suppose that those readers of the future are us, those who were born fifteen or twenty years after his death, in a world very different from and in many ways worse than the one he knew. But maybe we are not his intended readers. On rereading, for example, some passages of *Umbral*, or the fantastic, fantastical and beautifully 'quantum' ending of *Yesterday*, I get the impression that Juan Emar wasn't even writing for us. Yes, we can read him and enjoy him and think we understand, but deep down we know his books will be read and enjoyed and understood better by readers in a time yet to come.

ALEJANDRO ZAMBRA, MEXICO CITY, 2021
Chilean poet, short-story writer and novelist

Yesterday

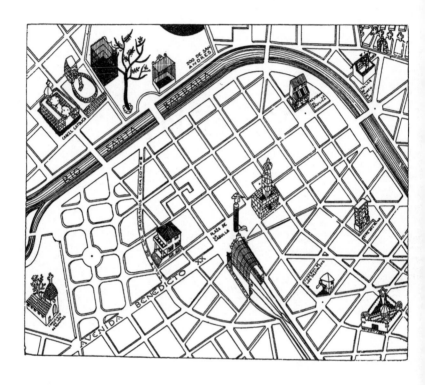

San Agustín de Tango: city of the Republic of Chile, on the banks of the Santa Barbara River, 32 degrees latitude south and 73 degrees longitude east; 622,708 inhabitants. Cathedral, basilica and archbishop. Manganese mines in the surroundings.

ILLUSTRATION BY GABRIELA EMAR

Yesterday morning, here in the city of San Agustín de Tango, I saw at long last the spectacle I had so yearned to see: a beheading. The victim was Rudecindo Malleco, poor fool, who was thrown in jail six months ago yesterday for what was judged to be an unpardonable crime.

Behold, his crime.

Rudecindo Malleco was a man like any other. And like all men, one fine day he got married. He chose as his mate the woman who today is his disconsolate widow, the sorrowful Matilde Atacama. On that very first night, Rudecindo Malleco received a most enjoyable surprise. He already knew from his friends that the whole matter would culminate in a quite remarkable pleasure, but never did he imagine such extremes. He found it all so delightful that he had to struggle to wrench himself from his wife's side, and when the lustful rascal walked down the street thinking of his Matilde, his smile was so lascivious that many a chaste young girl blushed in shame.

But you see, the years passed for poor Rudecindo with the same inexorable speed as they do for all the citizens of this city or any other, and, as is natural, the good man began to feel his strength affected.

In the beginning, Delight had smiled on him non-stop. After a time, however, he found it necessary to invoke Lady Delight's name less often. Later, he had to resign himself to the fact that Delight – ever more arrogant a lady – would visit when she, and not he, thought it best. And at last, he found that, except for the first and fifteenth days of each month, the great lady was doubtless occupied on other errands, for she did not come knocking at his door.

I believe it goes without saying that as the good man's impotence increased, so too did his sadness. Our good Malleco became melancholy, his character turned black, and many are those who claim to have caught him weeping to himself. Had things continued in this vein, I don't doubt that Rudecindo's name would be yet another on the list of suicides. But no. His very sadness saved him. True, one might say it also led him to the ultimate punishment, but even so, it did save him from suicide and grant him several more years of intense pleasure.

One night, our neurasthenic hero found himself drinking a beer alone in a corner of the Barefoot Tavern. It was the second day of the month and so he saw stretched out before him a long, sad wait. Suddenly, an old friend not seen in years.

(I should state a point in Malleco's favour: never, throughout the whole process, did he reveal the identity of this friend, thus making it impossible for the authorities to nab his accomplice.)

Well. They sat down together, the beer flowed, their tongues untied and good Rudecindo thought it opportune to confide his misfortunes in the hope of some sound advice.

And confide he did. He believed his friend would pity him, but to his surprise, this friend didn't see Malleco's weakness as a disgrace. Quite the opposite, in fact: the friend assured him things were actually much better just as they were, and that the whole problem could be resolved simply by replacing quantity with quality. And it seems that until very late that night he advised Malleco, instructed him, explaining things in such a wealth of detail that Rudecindo left that tavern happy as could be and convinced, utterly convinced, that with intelligence, with cunning, with shrewdness, with refinement – let us cut to the chase: that with their *minds* participating in the act, Rudecindo and Matilde would reach unsuspected pleasures, so intense and long-lasting they would easily fill the icy half-month of waiting.

That very night Rudecindo told Matilde his new ideas, and as of that precise moment they began to anticipate – brimming, overflowing with sensuality – the fifteenth of that month.

The fifteenth came. Their wait was crowned with success. Both minds participated wildly, and Rudecindo and Matilde reached the very pinnacle of all delight.

From that moment on they lived starry-eyed with pleasure. Their very lives became remembrance and evocation.

But Rudecindo Malleco was, first and foremost, a good person. Never had selfishness taken root in his soul. Believing himself in possession of the secret of love, Rudecindo Malleco wanted to share it with others like him. He began straight away to freely tell anyone who would listen that the pleasures of love exist in the mind and not outside it. Big mistake, friends, big mistake!

While it's true that many people thought the idea was good and adopted it for their own personal use, it's also true that for others the advice went in one ear and out the other, and it's no less true that to many, many people the thing seemed scandalous, they thought it went against nature, they judged the idea to be diabolical. And so it was that very soon an evil whisper began to surround poor Rudecindo. There was gossip and old ladies peeked out of their windows when the man walked down the street. People spoke in low voices about corruption, excess and dark degradations. Public opinion entered the fray and allusions were made between newspaper lines. In the end, the murmurings and discontent were such that the law thought it necessary to take a stand on the issue.

One morning, two guards appeared at poor Rudecindo's home and begged him to be so kind as to accompany them.

The doors of the prison closed behind good Rudecindo Malleco.

One can imagine the formidable scandal this produced.

The enemies of love's celebration rejoiced and sang hallelujah, but the friends of love cried foul to the heavens above. And in response to the voices of the first, who clamoured for vice to be punished, the second decried this violation of individual rights. Soon, this second group collected enough money to hire a first-rate lawyer for the hapless Malleco: the young and talented Felipe de Tarapacá.

No sooner did this man take over poor Rudecindo's defence than things began to turn in his favour.

Tarapacá contended: 'Why has Citizen Rudecindo Malleco been arrested and jailed? Of what crime is he accused? Is it the case that lascivious thoughts are crimes that should be punished? I ask the honourable court to cite one single article of our law or that of any civilized nation that entitles the authorities to intrude into the thoughts of a citizen during his legitimate coitus! Justice exercises its power over actions, nothing more than actions. Only when there is an action that falls under its claws can it cast its eyes upon the thoughts that motivated it. I give you the example of premeditation: premeditation is an aggravating circumstance only if an action later validates it. If the action does not happen, the circumstance is neither here nor there. Which of us or even of you, Honourable Judges, has not said to himself, upon seeing an enemy go by: "May lightning strike him down!" But since we all, yourselves included, continue on our way without provoking a flash of any kind, the law does not intervene. I ask you, of what act is Citizen Rudecindo Malleco guilty? Is there indisputable proof that my client has ever had relations with any woman besides the one given to him by law? If such had been the case, the law could intervene under the adultery statute. But not even then could a case be built around the more or less obscene thoughts that the culprit may have had before, during or after the act. And so I ask, Chief Justice, why is he being held in prison?'

In any case, Tarapacá's statement went something like that; clearly, it was all said with an eloquence and depth of knowledge that I will not for an instant attempt to reproduce here. What I mean to say is that the judges felt the whole thing becoming quite a pickle; that no one could justify the unhappy man's imprisonment, that Malleco's friends were shouting their theories ever louder, that the opinion of the indifferent masses was turning in his favour as his enemies fell silent, feeling they had no legal basis on which to oppose him. In sum, long story short, the prison doors were going to open for Citizen Rudecindo Malleco.

But here arose another voice, vibrant and incensed: the imposing voice of the Archbishop of San Agustín de Tango.

Monsignor contended: 'While it is true that the impious Tarapacá has contemplated the no less impious Malleco's case from the point of view of the laws fashioned by men here below, and has not found in them any charge that would impute guilt, it is even more true that man is not only the law that he himself fashions, he is also divine law, he is this law made flesh, he is the very reflection of the law of Our Father who art in heaven. And those who drag us through the muck of impiety and ignorance know full well that not only might acts be sinful, but also our consciences should be pure, and pure should our hearts be. And so it is that any immoral thoughts, desires or intentions, hidden though they may be from the eyes of man, are offensive to Our Father and glorify Lucifer. And I ask you, my brothers, is it possible to set a man free because he did not directly offend his peers, when he has, instead, offended God? Is this not to proclaim and affirm that man, vile worm, is superior to He who gave him life? And I wonder even further: if one of you offends his own aged father, is this not an offence against all of your brothers? Would any one of you allow a brother to offend your father? This, however, is the sad, regrettable spectacle that the law of man would offer us: to accept from this vile worm the most abominable offences to our Common Father, our Eternal Father. My brothers, we must all unite and plead for the impious and sinful Malleco to remain in prison, that he may be judged and punished!'

I have to give the same caveat here as I did for Tarapacá. Monsignor spoke with an eloquence and depth of knowledge that I would try in vain to reproduce. But, in the end, the sense of his words was more or less what I have recorded here.

The case returned, then, to court and the public waited in excitement. Half the city applauded; half the city protested.

Well, the court did not allow its arm to be twisted. It held fast within a fortress of legal codes, demonstrated that its mission could not diverge from the dictates of those laws, and confirmed the imprisoned citizen's freedom.

One radiant morning, the prison doors opened and there on the threshold, exultant, appeared the good Rudecindo Malleco. But scarcely had he taken three free steps down the street towards his adored Matilde than he was approached by two sextons, who handcuffed him and begged him to be so kind as to accompany them.

And so it was that five minutes after the doors of the Legal Prison of San Agustín de Tango had opened before him, the doors of the same city's Catholic Prison were closed behind him.

And the second trial began.

His defender was Father Benito del Crucifijo. I'll be brief: this trial did not and could not have many possible outcomes. The accusers' authority was crushing for sweet Father Benito. He himself, deep down, believed the hapless

Malleco to be guilty. The accusers numbered everyone minus one, and this one, as I have said, also thought him guilty. Thus the defence was limited to a prayer asking God to have mercy on this fallen, sinful man and, once the prayer was finished, Rudecindo Malleco was unanimously declared guilty.

But here, before proceeding to the punishment, a council had to be formed. A matter was in need of deliberation. What would the culprit's penalty be? It seems, according to the rumours that spread through the city, that since for every bishop there was a different opinion, they could reach no agreement. Finally, they found themselves forced to seek enlightenment from outside the council, and here indeed all were content to go and ask the holiest, the purest, the wisest in the entire Church: the Pious Reverend Carbuncle the All-Knowing.

Reverend Carbuncle the All-Knowing heard the bishops in silence. Then he smiled beatifically. Then he crossed himself. Finally, lowering his gaze, he recited: 'And if thy right eye offend thee, pluck it out and cast it from thee, for it is profitable for thee that one of thy members should perish and not that thy whole body should be cast into Hell. And if thy right hand offend thee, cut it off and cast it from thee, for it is profitable for thee that one of thy members should perish and not that thy whole body should be cast into Hell.'

The bishops reconvened. After the words of the wise Reverend All-Knowing, no doubt remained: the sinner must be amputated from the member that had occasioned his fall from grace.

Yes! Very good! But which member was this?

The council debated for another week. Finally, they opted to put it to a vote. There were eighty-eight voters. Those who voted that the head was the direct cause of the crime, forty-five. They based their vote on the fact that, from the start, the archbishop's words had implied that actions themselves were not the purview of the Church, as these had been taken over – seized, more accurately – by the justice of man; instead, the thoughts giving rise to said actions were the Church's jurisdiction. In any case, forty-five was one more than half, so there was nothing further to discuss.

Rudecindo Malleco would lose his head in the public square.

Hardly did I hear the sentence than I set out to traverse the city and call on my friends and acquaintances. After a thousand comings and goings, I managed to get two tickets to attend the execution. And so it was that yesterday, very early, very early indeed, my wife and I left our house and made our way to the place of punishment.

Here I should mention a few fairly curious observations. Or perhaps they are curious only to me, because of my previous state of ignorance. In any case, here goes.

When the bishops said 'public square', I imagined it would be exactly that, as when one says, for example, Chasuble Square here, or Puerta del Sol in Madrid, or Trafalgar Square in London and so on. It's true that in France they use the same expression, and in Paris, at least, the square is a boulevard, Boulevard Arago if I remember correctly. I should have realized that, in these matters, square could mean anywhere. But I did not, and so I was surprised to find that the deed would be done in a place very much like an outdoor circus: there was a short, circular barricade and, inside that barricade, a ring of sawdust. The only appreciable difference from a classic circus was that the ring, instead of being round, was long and oval.

We quickly found our seats, settled in comfortably and continued to examine the place. On the right side of the ring there was a wall, in the middle of which was a low, narrow doorway, through which a stone staircase was visible. Of this staircase I could see some eight or nine steps from my seat, no more. The lintel hid the rest from view. I don't know what was to the left; it didn't occur to me to look that way, or if I did – and I now think this is more likely – I didn't pay much attention to it. In any case, I can say for certain that that side of the arena was much darker than the rest. In the ring, next to the door and at the foot of the staircase, they had placed the guillotine. I had always imagined guillotines – perhaps because of the terror they inspire in me – to be of gigantic proportions. Not so. At least, the one they'd set up there in the ring was quite small. Another thing I observed, which seemed to show great consideration for poor Rudecindo, was that the four or five lamps that lit the place had been covered with black crêpe.

We must have been there no more than fifteen minutes when a murmur among the spectators warned me that the hour of the gory deed drew near. I looked towards the staircase. On it, descending, a soldier's boots appeared.

The boots paused, one next to the other on the steps, and at their side landed the butt of a rifle. 'Surely,' I thought, 'the soldier is here to hold back the crowd that will rush to go up the stairs to see Rudecindo.' I was correct. A second later, on the step below the boots, two thick shoes with hobnail soles appeared; then some patent-leather ankle boots; then some tennis shoes; then some small shoes with towering heels; then... oh, I give up! A whole crowd. And we continued waiting in silence, until I heard the screech of a spring suddenly set in motion. We all looked above the door, where we saw a tiny window, and once the screeching sound reached its highest note, the two shutters flew open and smacked against the stones of the wall. A little wooden bird appeared and cried: 'Cuckoo!' and disappeared again.

This was the exact moment of Rudecindo Malleco's entrance. He wore a white shirt and black trousers and his hands were tied behind his back. Following him, the executioner, dressed in the same way, gently pushed him with the index finger of his left hand. At Rudecindo's side was a small friar, all in black, lively, sprightly, who talked and talked to the condemned man. I recognized sweet Father Benito del Crucifijo, but I couldn't hear what he was saying. My wife couldn't hear either. They reached the miniature guillotine – I call it so, for I cannot believe there are no larger ones – and poor Rudecindo fell flat on his face.

And here, please allow me another observation: the way things occur in reality is very different from the way they are generally said to happen. We believed that next to that infernal device there would be a solemn man in frock coat and top hat who would pull a lever with a decisive gesture, the way it's always said to happen. None of that. It was the executioner himself who with his own hands took up the knife and dealt a ferocious downward blow to the poor devil's neck. His body fell to one side, and to my great stupefaction I saw that it continued breathing, breathing hard, like an athlete after strenuous exercise. Meanwhile, the head had rolled away. The blow had not been masterful; quite the contrary. For the knife, though it had penetrated at the base of the cranium, had exited just above the eyes, which therefore remained in the victim's possession. Or perhaps this was due to the sentence itself, which called for the amputation of the sinful part and nothing more – in this instance, of the thinking matter. If that was the case, we should congratulate the executioner on his extreme artistry.

What followed was a somewhat grotesque and even pitiful spectacle. Father Benito, as the piece of head began to roll, ran after it, picked it up as one would a watermelon rind and, after examining it quickly, dropped it back on the ground. Rudecindo took that chance to pick it up himself and put it where it had always been. It didn't fit exactly, no. The cut was perfectly visible and the good man was left with the ridiculous air of one wearing a too-small hat. And then things went from bad to worse. Rudecindo, always on the ground – he must not have had the strength to stand up – began to curse the executioner and, not content with that, to threaten him with his fists. The latter did not heed the threats and remained by the guillotine, and only after a long while did he turn and advance towards his victim, pretending – in jest, to be sure, purely in fun – to accept the fistfight. But the executed Malleco must have thought that he genuinely accepted the challenge, for he turned over on his back like a cornered animal and began to flap his four extremities in a desperate windmill. The executioner dropped his hands, shrugged his shoulders two or three times and, smiling at the audience, returned to his guillotine. Just then, Rudecindo Malleco entered the throes of death. Two minutes later, he had passed.

I began to feel very low. The weight of the blood spilled in the ring seemed to fall onto me. I said to my wife: 'Enough already of executions, guillotines and all the rest! Let's get out of here! Let's go!'

'Yes,' she replied. 'Enough already. Let's go!'

And we left through a side gate that an elegant groom, after bowing several times, opened for us.

We went out onto the street under a damp, grey sky. We had planned to visit the San Andrés Zoo, so off we went in that direction.

In itself, to tell the truth, I didn't find the zoo much deserving of its fame – very few of the creatures there were worthy of attention. Let's see: the fourteen lionesses were so-so, the monkeys a bit more so, and very much so, I can't deny it, was the ostrich. But, beyond these, the rest left me cold.

The lionesses were interesting primarily because of the role one of them would soon come to play, but also because of the utter uniformity of their movements, as if they were propelled by a single spring hidden from our eyes. And as I imagined the real possibility of this spring, I also had to imagine someone beside it, activating the movements that would then manifest in the she-lions themselves.

Thinking thus, the following phrase came to me spontaneously and stuck fast: 'Fourteen she-lions secretly moved by a secret spring the he-lion moves.'

I brought my lips to my wife's left ear and whispered this phrase.

She looked at me sidelong and whispered: '*Littérateur.*'

Whatever the case, their uniformity rose to a level of majesty. As we drew closer to the trench that encircled the vast space reserved for them, the fourteen she-lions slept – on the ground or on rocks or teetering in the trees – they slept, I say, in the exact same pose. After a minute they all flicked their tails once, not more. After another minute they stretched, yawning and showing their claws, after which they got up and shook themselves the way dogs do when they leave the water. Then, suddenly, they all turned their heads our way and stared at us with an utter, petrifying fixity. And then a very strange thing happened. Up until that moment the zoo had been full of the various sounds of other caged animals, and the birds, the wind in the trees and even the city nearby. Of human noises there were none, as my wife and I were the only people there. And, well, when the lionesses looked at us, all sound ceased, down to the tiniest whisper, a black, absolute silence fell over us and we were paralysed. In that silence, the twenty-eight rays from those eyes pierced our bodies so cleanly and easily that both of us felt, from our heads to our feet, fourteen sharp, strident little pains as they bored through us and drove into the earth some distance behind us. This began to be intolerable.

'Let's go, let's go!' I said to my wife. 'If we carry on like this, bits of lion-gaze will be left circulating in our blood, and we cannot let that happen, since we still have, my darling, many things left to do in this life.'

'Very true,' she replied. 'Let's go!'

We fled, disturbed and almost frightened. Only when we reached the trench that separated us from the monkeys did we regain our calm. A high rock had been set up in the centre of their enclosure, a very high and steep rock indeed, on which the monkeys climbed, ran around, jumped and climbed some more. There were hundreds of monkeys, all belonging to the cynocephalus family, though they seemed smaller than animals of that genus I had seen before. They looked happy to be right where they were. Some of them, between one leap and another, hungrily gobbled handfuls of peanuts; others had brief scuffles; some couples mated. In short, the usual life led by such creatures. I remember one who sat down facing us, dignified, then turned its big, dog-like head in profile and urinated profusely.

The day was still grey and dark. We were about to continue our walk when a beam of sunlight broke through the clouds and bathed the entire rock in its glow. What a magnificent, splendid sight we beheld then! The hundreds of monkeys paused, amazed, and looked up at the sun and opened their mouths disproportionately wide, and then they burst out in a splendid song.

It started with a single note, just one, and then the song climbed upward, rocking softly like a roller coaster, and when it reached its highest point it turned sharp, shrill and savage. At that point, the monkeys stood on their hind legs and raised their arms to the sun. Then the song started its descent, and once it reached its lowest point, the sound it produced became cavernous, like the tumbling of subterranean rocks. The monkeys then bent to stand on four legs, which shook like springs and made their bodies tremble fast. From there the ascent started again, long, long, and the creatures began to stand erect, and it seemed to us that we were held aloft in the air by invisible, hairy hands. And then after a moment, at the song's most piercing point, downward, downward! Once more, the long way down. The sun shone. Now up again. Now down.

My wife elbowed me and, indicating the monkeys with her eyes, she motioned to me that I should do as they, and she, did. My wife sang. A round and blue contralto, a windpipe of soft velvet – that is my wife's voice. Parallel, exactly parallel to the roller coaster of the cynocephali's voices, only a third lower, she added her sweet, husky voice. And roller coaster and windpipe then set out together to spiral through the air, cavorting with the beam of sunlight in magnificent harmony. I was held captive by the thousand cynocephali and the interminable note of my wife's voice beneath theirs. But a second dig from her elbow called me to my duty. I took a deep breath, filling my lungs with fresh air, yes, very fresh, except that, with a certain wisdom, I chose to mix in a bit of monkey-scent and a hint of my life companion's perfume. That way, I was all tangled up in that splendid sound and, after clearing my throat, I managed to emit a sound a fifth higher than the monkeys' song with my limpid tenor voice. And we all rocked through the air on our vibrations: the monkeys holding on to each other on their roller coaster; I, higher up with my flat, silvery voice; below, cementing everything together, my wife and the blue velvet of her serene windpipe.

We went down. For me, so much better than going up. But soon a fear for my wife began to fill me. Oh, vain fear! Oh, blessed woman of mine! May my admiration for you be forever stamped upon these pages! As the thousand creatures set off a formidable avalanche of subterranean rocks, as I myself descended hundreds of metres below the earth's surface, my wife, defying and demolishing all, went down with incredible agility, respecting the same agreement she had made in the middle of the journey when she began to sing, so that, to the monkeys' inferno, to my own clay substrate, she added the majestic sliding of deep waters that have never seen the sun's light and are emptied into the earth's entrails through caverns that none of us will ever see, save for when she revealed them to us through her song.

Another ascent began. Soon we reached the surface of the earth. We went up. Now I was flooded with fear for myself. The monkeys could easily reach their highest, shrillest stridency, but I don't believe there is a human voice in the world that could equal such heights. What to say of my own! I began to tremble like a child. I was defenceless. I was going first, at the apex, crowned by the sun, my skin pricked by sharp knives of cold air in our prodigious ascent. And I felt at my back the keen whistle from the thousand throats of the cynocephali driving me pitilessly onward. And behind, far behind, in desperation, I heard the murmur of my companion's low voice, far, far away from me. But yet again, as so often in my life, my wife came generously to my aid. My voice was at its highest point. The others, as they pushed, were starting to needle me as I resisted reflexively. Then my wife indicated to me where her own note was, then the monkeys', then finally – and here was my salvation – the space that was left between them. A quick wink from her begged me to throw myself from my heights without hesitation and into that harmony-preserving space. But how? Would there be a place for me? Or, in trying to find it, would I destroy the song, causing it to erupt into the most gnashing dissonance?

No. It was only a question of sharpening and tuning my ears in a different way, and the three voices would span half the original distance between the highest and lowest notes – my wife always below, me now huddled in the middle and the monkeys at the apex. And our three voices would continue in a different harmony, a different existence, climbing up towards the sun.

All it took was the decision. I threw my flat, silver voice downward; I collided with the thousand sharp points of air ascending; there was a brief snapping sound like metal hitting the ocean; and I continued falling, nearly reaching the velvet pipes of my beloved. But quickly she helped me find – aided also by my newly tuned ears – just the right position for my voice, and, fearless now, comforted with her behind me, protected in front by the monkeys' cold knives of air, we went on in a harmony never before heard, we went on, spellbound, absorbed, reaching the furthest point beyond which there is no music, no discrete sound – no individual sounds, you might say, as ours were – where everything, all existence, was one single and absolute music.

A cloud passed. The sun disappeared. Our voices plunged like injured birds from those fantastic heights and disappeared, dead, back down our throats. We fell mute in the new grey.

Many monkeys urinated. Some hit each other. One couple mated. Others gobbled handfuls of peanuts.

'Let's go!' I said to my wife. 'Let's go! Enough already of cynocephali!'

'Yes, enough,' she said. 'Let's go.'

Behind some tall palm trees, strutting from here to there, from side to side, dignified, magnificent: a strong and beautiful ostrich.

In spite of its strength and beauty, we chose to continue our walk. My thoughts were more or less along these lines: 'What could an ostrich matter to me? Looking at it might perhaps be pleasant, even delightful, but why would such a bird bring delight to a man like me? Why? Why?' And this question of mine sounded gloomy in that vast garden. It was better to keep going. To stop would be to ask the question again, to ask it would be to rack my brains until I found an answer. Oh, how many shadowy meditations did I see looming in my future if I let even a single drop of delight fall upon my soul as I gazed at that magnificent creature! From then on, I would have to devote all my moments of repose, all my moments of distraction, all my moments of reading and study, all my moments of love and sensuousness, all of it, I would have to devote to finding the solution to this problem: 'What happens in the depths of a man, what unconsciousness awakens within him – what remote echoes of God before creation or messages of a future in God after creation – to bring forth the spark of delight that wells up at the poised step of an ostrich?' I understood that I would be snatched up in the claws of abstraction and never again would I have enough peace in my heart to wander free of worry through the streets, eat with gusto, or sleep side by side with the precious other half of my soul.

We had to continue our walk.

But at that very moment a cry of horror thundered through the air.

'The lioness! The lioness!'

I screamed: 'Help!'

And my wife: 'Jesus!'

I saw – though I'd believed the zoo deserted – thousands of human beings running frantically, possessed by panic. Men, women, old people, children, soldiers, priests: it was an electric stampede, while from one end of the place, and growing ever louder, came the terrifying roars of the escaped she-lion.

Paralysed by terror, we couldn't move. But suddenly I saw, shooting through the sky like a projectile above the treetops, the terrible lioness in the midst of a menacing leap.

And there my clear memories end.

Next comes a dark point of which I know nothing. My wife doesn't either. And then the clearness of my perception returned.

We were at the furthest top of a giant elm tree, mute, pale and trembling. How we climbed up there, what strength and agility propelled us, as I say, neither I nor my wife knows.

Around us, as far as our eyes could see, men, women, old people, children, soldiers and priests were running and running. The she-lion was descending from the sky, claws and teeth bared. At our feet, undaunted, dignified, magnificent, the beauteous ostrich continued its dancing promenade.

This was the most acute moment of suspense, of tension, that my wife and I had ever experienced. I could calculate the curve of the lioness's descent, and she was going to alight right in the bird's domain.

And so it was. The she-lion landed. The ostrich stopped. One facing the other. There were no more than fifteen metres between them.

Oh, my dear, beloved wife, why must I love you so?

And then it happened, the appalling thing.

But not yet, because before it occurred, the lioness crouched down, flicked her tail briskly, flattened her ears, narrowed her eyes, bared her teeth, growled like a volcano, and repeated all those actions several times.

Simultaneously, the ostrich, faced with such a horrific display, did nothing but gracefully stretch its neck and wait with half-closed eyes.

Wait!

A hellish word for me and for my wife, though not for the women, men, old people, children, soldiers and priests, who went madly on with their running, running, running.

Our wait lasted… well, that depends on whether the time was measured by chronometers or by us ourselves.

Contained in that moment of waiting were all the manvantaras that compose our earthly cycles, our systems and whatever comes after.

When suddenly it happened, the appalling thing: the enraged lioness attacked.

She attacked with another menacing leap. When she leapt into the air, the leaves of the giant elm tree shuddered and rustled, the mosquitoes sheltered within them took flight, and all the world over, every aeroplane in existence shot up vertically in a splendid soar.

Then the lioness began to execute her fatal semicircle through the air that would land her exactly on top of the bird, crushing and ripping it to pieces.

The semicircle to be drawn was drawn. The semicircle's destiny was fulfilled: the lioness leapt upon the ostrich.

Here, I beg the reader to please follow me carefully. What happened was the following. But first, I must explain what would have happened if what happened had not happened; that is to say, if the ostrich had remained immobile. If things had gone like that, the she-lion, thanks to her semicircle's precision, would have fallen right on top of the ostrich and, upon falling, she would have destroyed it in an instant. But that did not happen. This is what happened.

When the tips of the lioness's front claws were precisely thirty-seven centimetres from the tip of the ostrich's beak, the latter executed a quick step to the right. But this step had something peculiar about it. If I knew how to draw, I would draw an ostrich just as it appeared before the step to the right, and then, in the same drawing, I would use a dotted line to draw the creature's position after the step. Unfortunately, I don't know how to draw. But, I repeat, if I did know how to draw, two ostrich bodies would be seen in the drawing, one at the centre of the paper, another to the side, to the right, and, finally, four feet belonging to the two. Up to now, nothing peculiar. But let us continue, and the peculiarity will come. The feet as well as bodies would be separate, clearly separate, as if belonging to two different creatures. But not so the necks, and even less so the heads. The neck of the first ostrich would be held straight up, that is to say perpendicular to the body; conversely, the one to the right would be inclined at an angle of forty-five degrees towards the first neck, in order to join up with it at more or less the middle of its length. As a result, there would be two bottom halves of the neck, but only one upper half and only one head. In other words, the ostrich launched both feet to the right, which brought the body with them, only part of the neck, and the head did not move: the head remained in the same place. As will be understood, if I have managed to express myself clearly, feet, body and lower part of the neck moved out of the lion's trajectory, while the upper part of the neck and the head remained within said area.

At that moment, gazing at the spectacle before us, I wanted to say to my wife: 'The ostrich's sideways movement has reminded me very clearly of the movement I saw Belmonte execute before a Veragua bull on 8 May 1920 in the Zaragoza ring, past 4.31 in the afternoon and before 4.32, when I was in the company of Lucrecia, the beautiful Lucrecia. Then, too, there was a step to the right, everything changing place except for the two hands and the cape, which remained in the bull's trajectory.'

Such was what I wanted to say, but I lacked the time, since I continued to formulate my thoughts and memories with the usual slowness of the citizens of San Agustín de Tango yesterday, which was the same usual, slow speed as the day before yesterday, as today and as tomorrow, as all the ages descended since Adam and all those yet to come, until the very last one wastes away. Conversely, the spectacle we witnessed and which evoked the memory of Belmonte was ruled by unheard-of speeds: not the speed of humans, but the breakneck speed of lions that are furthermore enraged, a compounded speed that surely compounded all existence, the spinning planets, moving constellations, the whole universe, except for the two of us, poor human beings stalled at the top of an elm, poor beings like so many others who roam and haunt this earth. Yes, ladies and gentlemen, like all who exist, for the men, women, children, old people, soldiers and priests had stopped their crazed running, and the magnificent universal aeroplanes had fulfilled their ascents and now flew, gliding like swans with no destination.

The thirty-seven centimetres were fulfilled. Then, at the first contact with the beast, the ostrich opened its beak immensely wide and we, thunderstruck and flabbergasted, observed from our perch the most astounding event that we had ever seen. The ostrich, I repeat, opened its beak incredibly wide, wider than I would ever have thought an ostrich beak could open, and the lioness, hurtling like fate itself, hurtled inside him, and in a thousandth of a second she disappeared.

She disappeared down the beak. She disappeared. Now with no dangerous she-lion on the loose, my wife and I clambered down from the elm and went to stand by the trench that encircled the bird's domain. From there we could watch the strange battle as it unfolded.

Within the ostrich's throat a large lump took shape. It remained motionless for a minute and then, slowly, it began to descend the length of the neck with several convulsions.

These convulsions brought to my mind the movements an enraged cat might make struggling inside a bag of gelatin.

I said as much to my wife. She cast over my brow a questioning glance. And with good reason, with quite good reason, since I don't think any mortal exists who has witnessed a cat going crazy inside a sack of gelatin, and if such a mortal does exist, I can assure you I am not him. And of this my wife was aware. Moreover, while it is true that there's a close resemblance between a lion and a cat, it is no less true that there's none between a bag of gelatin and a long ostrich neck covered in feathers, no matter how many lumps may take shape within them. My wife's silent questioning, then, was doubly justified. But what could I do? It was – to me, anyway – a cat imprisoned in gelatin and struggling heroically. Is it my fault? I answered her questioning glance with a silent appeal for forgiveness. She then took her eyes from my brow and we both turned our attention back to the bird.

The she-lion went down very slowly. At times, through the feathers, we could make out her four legs and her snout as she fought desperately to break free of the tube that had inhaled her and now held her prisoner. Will she make it? Will she not? These were the questions we were asking ourselves when, suddenly, there was no more room for doubt: she won't make it, no! If the poor beast had had any hope of bringing her work to a gainful end, no doubt the ostrich would have realized it, and an expression of fear or at least disquiet would have shown on its face. And there was none. Much to the contrary. As the fifteenth convulsion occurred, when the lump was at the middle of the neck, the ostrich smiled. Then, at the sixteenth, its smile turned into a soft chuckle, faltering and hesitant. There could be no doubt that the efforts of the beast inside it were giving it a slight tickle. And there was no doubt, either, that said tickle was increasing, since by the eighteenth convulsion the bird was giggling, giggling freely, and at the twenty-first, unable to contain itself any more, it burst out in a roar of laughter.

Before such a spectacle as this, she who is the companion of my very soul could not contain herself either, and a 'ha! ha! ha!' burst forth into the air as she clutched her ribs with her little hands of delicate marble. And upon seeing how both of them, the bird and my beloved, were laughing, I in turn let out the most thunderous, the most formidable peal of laughter that any human has ever laughed.

It was stupendous. The three of us hooted uncontrollably, rolling on the ground in peals of laughter that were more like howls, holding the pits of our stomachs, we with both our hands, the bird with its feet, shedding copious tears, our laughter resounding through the air as we choked and kicked our feet, all of us caught up, enveloped, surrounded by the same infernal and delirious joy.

How long? Who knows! We were conscious of nothing but our laughter. The only thing I know is that when the lion-lump reached the base of the ostrich's neck, there was one final shudder as the beast passed into the body proper of the bird. And… silence. The creature grew serene atop its long legs, calm and motionless as if meditating. We pursed our lips and, equally dignified, we waited.

The hands of the clocks traversed a fourth of a circle in the world's total stillness.

The nearby bell of Los Jerónimos sounded with a coppery ring, cleaving the calm in two. The bird sneezed. Then I sneezed. Finally, my sainted wife closed the cycle of sneezes by sneezing in turn.

And life went on.

Here began another phase of this strange battle. The ostrich took up a curious though familiar posture.

'It's going to defecate,' I murmured softly into my wife's ear.

'Quiet,' she responded.

And without exchanging a word, our arms linked, we walked over and stationed ourselves just behind the bird; that is, right in front of its tail.

And once more, we waited.

Our wait soon paid off. The tail feathers shook for a moment and then opened into a magnificent flower. Then the circle that appeared began to dilate and we, with indescribable happiness, saw the she-lion's snout appear from within. And she came sliding out. We saw her nose, her eyes – closed at first, they blinked and opened – her forehead, her ears, her neck. We had the feeling we were watching the eye of heaven rise on a splendid morning. My wife applauded vigorously.

At the sound of her hands, the lioness realized we were there and threw us an irate glance. I made a face at her and my wife stuck out her tongue. This was enough to anger the animal more, and she began to struggle to get her shoulders and front legs out. But the ostrich was on guard. When it felt that its prisoner might escape, it squeezed its orifice tight, so tight that the lioness cried out: 'Eeeeeeh!'

But she continued in spite of the pain. The ostrich continued as well. What we witnessed then was simply appalling. Behold.

The lioness, thanks to her consummate strength, emerged – slowly, yes, but she emerged. The ostrich, thanks to his own strength, also consummate, held on to the she-lion's skin with the pressure of his sphincter. As such, we saw appear, little by little, a lioness with a normal head and a beautiful pelt, but from the neck down she was skinned, terrifyingly skinned. She got one paw out, then the other, like someone taking a hand from a plush glove, or more like – if seen from inside the bird – someone pressing open the peel of a ripe banana and expelling its aromatic pulp. Horror! Her entire torso came out of the ostrich that way, and likewise her hind legs. And there she stood, held only by her tail. And then, with a supreme effort, a sonorous, sharp lash, she managed to dislodge it, and we had before our eyes the most hair-raising and macabre she-lion one could ever imagine. Blood dripped from her whole body and the drops, when they hit the grass, produced the distant murmur of a morning rain. Then she broke out in a sweat, a greenish sweat that made it seem for a moment as if she was wrapped in a layer of celluloid. But this sweat fell all at once, explosive, with the sound of an oar falling flat on the surface of a calm sea. And the blood came back and the sweat came back and the whole time the poor animal gazed up at the skies. Until finally, without further ado, she started to run like crazy. We saw her vanish through the foliage and we watched as her gory body disappeared. Then, when the very tip of her tail was gone, we dragged our gazes back along the trail of greenish blood left behind in her flight; we dragged our eyes, that is, back to the magnificent ostrich's behind.

It had closed, and the creature was distractedly watching the flitting of the birds. But then, noticing us, it winked an eye our way. We stopped. The bird then turned its long neck around, inserted its beak inside itself, grabbed hold of its victim's pelt and with admirable mastery removed it. The bird spread the pelt out on the ground and flattened it nicely with its two large feet. Lying down on one half, it covered itself up to the nose with the other and closed its eyes. A minute later it was sound asleep.

I looked at my wife and she looked at me.

'Let's go!' I said. 'Let's go! Enough already of lions and ostriches.'

'Yes,' she replied. 'Enough already. Let's go!'

The bronze bells of Los Jerónimos tolled noon.

We were hungry.

We headed for the Basilica restaurant, which was the closest, and sat down at a table.

My wife ordered:

>Pickled duck.
>Goat stew.
>Blood sausages with mashed potatoes.
>Lucuma fruit with cream.

I ordered:

>Pork roll.
>Conger eel soup.
>*Cochayuyo* seaweed with onion.
>*Picarones* in sugar sauce.

Afterwards we both had a coffee.

'Did you pay?' she asked.

'I paid,' I replied.

'Are we off, then?'

'We're off.'

And we left.

The clouds – which some hours earlier had opened up a sliver and brought a song from the cynocephali, my wife and me; which had then closed to make us fall silent; which had grown transparent to shine a bright though tempered light onto the ferocious brawl; and which had finally withdrawn during lunch to help us devour our courses to the music of golden rays – had now grown heavy and dark again, and distilled into a confused fog that made of San Agustín de Tango an inhospitable metropolis, sticky and blue.

We walked laboriously, startled by the silhouettes of the street lights. Where to go? For a while we followed a random pedestrian until a bus or tram stopped us, putting too much mist between us and him, and we lost him. Then we turned, alternating right and left, after something, anything. But nothing. Where to go?

When, suddenly, an idea: we should go and see our friend, the painter Rubén de Loa, on Immaculate Conception Street.

We headed that way.

Rubén de Loa's studio is located off the second court-yard on the ground floor of a fairly gloomy building. The light from the window filters in through climbing vines whose leaves are always in motion. The leaves turn the light green. The frosted glass turns the green aquatic.

That is the place that we entered.

Rubén de Loa was painting. What is more, for twenty-four years Rubén de Loa had been painting non-stop. When he saw us over the top of his canvas, he came towards us. We, out of courtesy, advanced towards him. And the three of us moved as if through water, smoothly lifting off from the floor and floating down again in slow motion.

He offered us a seat. He sat there, my wife here, and I sat across from them, in the middle.

I said: 'Your studio is too green, Rubén de Loa.'

'Greenish,' he corrected me.

'Aquatic,' my wife emphasized.

We fell silent, all three of us smoking.

Then, through the smoke rings, I began to examine my dear old friend.

Because of the reflected green of the vines, his long black hair looked like neglected autumn grass. His jaguar features remained unchanged. His skin was still firm. To be sure, he is still young. He is thirty-one years old, given that he has painted for twenty-four years and that he has painted since he was seven. His gaze was ninety per cent inward. The remaining ten per cent, as it poured out of him, was a little hollow and very kind. He smoked a pipe, as a painter should. He did not sneeze or cough. Only every quarter of an hour he would say: 'Well, well, well.'

To which I would respond: 'Yes, sir.'

And my wife: 'That's how it goes.'

After an hour, Rubén de Loa began to look at she who is my better half. I followed suit. She looked transparent, like a small tomb. Her hair, brown in the streets of San Agustín de Tango, now took on the green of the studio and the sight of it started to make me feel nauseous. But such was not the case for my dear old friend, who looked at her always and longed for her.

Then I looked at my hands, wanting to see some living part of me as well in that studio. They were likewise suffering the window's effects, which plunged me into a deep meditation on death.

My meditation was uninterrupted except, very infrequently, by my friend's 'Well, well, well' and my wife's 'That's how it goes.' Until, partially returning to life, I wondered: 'What *is* this "it" that goes?'

I thought that it could be nothing other than Rubén de Loa's sinful desire. And then I thought a change of subject would be wise. I started right in on the art of good painting, saying to my friend: 'You're headed in the wrong direction, Rubén de Loa.'

In speaking this way, not for an instant, not even deep down inside, was I referring to his sinful desire. It was a sincere statement directed solely at his art, or more accurately at the atmosphere in which his art came to be, since, in all honesty, he had shown us nothing yet of his work, and the last canvas of his I had seen was from five years prior. I was speaking, then, of the atmosphere. Let that be perfectly clear.

'You're headed in the wrong direction, Rubén de Loa, for you live and work in an artificial atmosphere. Nothing that is done exclusively under the influence of the colour green can turn out well. This is less a studio than the depths of a jungle, or – even worse! – it's how we imagined the jungle's depths as children. I've spent this whole long hour surprised by the silence in here, for I kept expecting to hear the cry of a macaw, the yelp of a white-eared possum, the whistle of an anteater. Is it possible to paint like this?'

'There is no danger,' answered Rubén de Loa. 'Of course this colour is not green, and it has nothing to do with the jungle. This is a grey-green, or better yet a greenish grey, and it has nothing of the jungle beyond the hue of a young eucalyptus – hardly green at all, hardly. And this hue, upon reflection, has just as much right to live as the bronze of sunny days or the violet of thunderstorms.'

'Let us compromise, my friend,' I continued. 'Your greenish grey, I cannot accept. Let us compromise on a greyish green, with the caveat that I have reservations about this latter term in particular. But you must admit, I'm compromising. Why don't you compromise a bit as well?'

'How so?' he asked indifferently.

'By cutting away those leaves that cover the window.'

Rubén de Loa let out a scornful laugh and asked me: 'Have you gone mad?'

He waited a minute and then, in a confidential tone, his gaze alternating between my wife and me, he told us: 'I am a lonely man. I have no wife or children or relatives or friends. I have no vices. If I smoke, it's out of habit and not for pleasure. I don't go to the theatre or cinema. I don't have affairs with women or men or beasts or objects. And work is hard for me, my work makes me suffer. And so, I do not know pleasure. I exaggerate. I know but one, one and only one. And this is given to me precisely by those leaves that you are asking me to cut. Sit here.'

Then to my wife: 'Madam, please sit here.'

Then to both of us: 'Let us look at the leaves. You will see that their shapes and their shadows, when they move in the breeze, cease to be leaves and become an infinite variety of fish swimming silently in a great green aquarium. See how they pass by, approach, move away, return, tap the glass, turn, disappear, reappear. Then I feel as though the water of the aquarium filters in through the window and, flooding everything, floods me as well. And I, in turn, am a fish. I swim languidly through the air, buoyed up on the smoke of my pipe. It is my only pleasure. You two forget that I am not a happy man.'

'Rubén de Loa,' I said, affectionately reaching out my hands to him, 'please accept our apologies. In truth, my wife and I are happy. We have relatives and friends, and many pleasures dwell between our sheets. My wife frequents the cinema; I, the athletic fields. Rubén de Loa, in our name and from the bottom of our hearts, we beg you never to cut even one of these leaves, and to always find delight in swimming through the air of your studio.'

Our good friend then embraced us tender-heartedly and, taking our hands in his, led us in a slow, slow, slow aquatic pirouette that shortened our breath a bit and filled us with delight when we felt our feet making contact once again, bit by bit, with the studio's floorboards.

We returned to our seats.

I said: 'Let us set aside the subject of the leaves. They belong to your private life and do not concern us. But aesthetics belong to us all, and so I must insist: greenish grey, greyish green, jungle or young eucalyptus, say it however you like, but it exerts an influence over you. You will see, my friend, that the day must come when you see blue as green, yellow as green, orange as green, and green to you will be black and white and any colour in existence. And such a thing is not sustainable; from seeing so much green, you will no longer see green itself. You can argue that it's better to know one thing to its core than to glide along the surface of a thousand. But I tell you, this here is not knowing, this is not to penetrate. This is reduction, believe me, Rubén de Loa. At this rate the day will come when you even see red as green.'

'Stop right there!' exclaimed Rubén de Loa. 'Stop there! Not another word!'

'Why?' I asked, surprised.

As he had done a moment earlier, our good friend waited a minute and then, looking at each of us in turn, he spoke to us in his confidential tone, to which he added a touch of sadness.

'Obviously you two are ignorant of the role red has in relation to green! Know this: red is the complement of green, and this law of complements is the most important thing in this world.'

I murmured: 'Hmmm!'

My wife widened her eyes a bit, then returned them to their normal state.

'Yes,' continued Rubén de Loa, 'it is incredibly important. For red, as the complement of green, complements it in all of life's circumstances. No, don't laugh! I'll explain. Whatever complements, balances; whatever balances, stabilizes. Very important, this making stable, because whatever stabilizes makes viable. Makes what viable? you will ask. Fair enough. I will explain. Makes viable the circulation of life through. Just that: through, t-h-r-o-u-g-h. Let us think about it for a moment, shake up our minds. Life circulates through; that is, it *can* circulate because it has something through which to do so. This is elementary. And it has this something thanks to the fact that there is, in that through which it circulates, a stability, and that stability is only possible thanks to a constant, or almost constant, balance, and for there to be a balance there must be at least two to balance. Just one – with what, with whom, would it balance? And for the balance of the two to continue, those two must create between them a complement. Let us say it straight out: they must complement each other. Otherwise, all is chaos, utter annihilation, a return to the day before the first day of creation. And in that case, there would be no you or your distinguished little wife, no me or my paintings, no anything else. On the other hand, as things stand now, as they are today, life circulates in a great balanced complement and I, poor Rubén de Loa, in the image of the Creator himself, can bestow total life, one more point, one more tube, I would say, through which it can enjoy circulating. That is what I do with my paintings here in my studio, my friends.'

And, saying this, he darted about into several corners of the room, and from under various pieces of furniture he took twelve paintings that he lined up against the wall opposite the window.

My wife and I were plunged into mute contemplation. Rubén de Loa came and stood behind us. He lifted both arms so that one of his hands was above each of our heads and in that pose, unmoving, unblinking, he kept watch over our mute contemplation.

Rubén de Loa's paintings were green.

Rubén de Loa's paintings contained every possible green. Those of all the hours of the day and of the night; those of all the years of history. They contained all the greens the earth has left behind in her eternal evolution, all those that are with her now, all that will latch onto her in her future revolutions. Those of the four elements. Those of ether. Those of life's gestation in an ovum, those of birthing and flourishing, those of plenitude, those created by the air inside a coffin as it is consumed. The green of silence, the green of murmurings, the green of pandemonium. The green of God. The green of Satan. All, all of them! Why go on? In their mere enumeration I would fill ten volumes and then, if I wanted to enumerate the relation of each green enumeration with all the others, a hundred volumes would not be enough. Moreover, is not the word 'all' sufficient? Let us fix that word firmly in our heads: all. All the greens. It is enough to say it like this. However, I don't know why, something like compunction drives me to go on with green examples, as if by not continuing I would fail to honour my friend's magnificent green talent. Yes, but where would I start the first line of the first page of the first volume? Let it suffice for me to say that there was my own green, which up till then I had not known existed. There was my wife's green. And the green of our friend. And the green of the relationship between my wife and me. And that of the relationship between my wife and him. And between him and me. And among the three of us at that point in time, because if we moved, it would be a different green, which could also be found in the paintings, the green of that exact place and time, and, just as no clock ever stops, so too the greens of Rubén de Loa's paintings, etc., a thousand times, etc. My God! Isn't the one word enough: ALL?

And still, I fear I don't do justice to his talents. So, since there is no way to enumerate them all, let us look, at least, as a tribute to him, at an anecdote that will demonstrate to what extent our friend's greens affected all that fell under their sway.

Behold.

While my wife and I were there contemplating the paintings, our friend behind us with his hands above us, a toucan belonging to an elderly woman next door burst into wild song. It should be mentioned that, having seen the bird on several previous occasions, I can attest that it belonged to the genus *Calyptocephallus gayi*; that is to say, a multicoloured toucan, but one without a single green feather.

Well then, that shrill song of exploding colours penetrated into the studio through the high window, crossed it at the normal speed and came to rest above our heads. Then, from there, it inflated roundly like a soap bubble and burst into a breeze that tousled our hair, while a greenish drizzle fell upon us and entered us first through our ears, then harmonized our eyes with the twelve paintings, leaving us feeling like we were submerged in a calm swamp of algae and still waters.

And this *should* suffice, but now I see that so far I have not gone beyond the world of the senses, the greens that can somehow or other be perceived by the senses. And so, allow me one more word.

The canvases held, as well, the greens that are imperceptible to the senses. I should explain. Rubén de Loa's theory on complements is doubtless very true; that is to say, in order for balance to be maintained and, consequently, for that which exists to exist, there must be – limiting ourselves to the case in point – for every amount of green produced, an equal amount of red, and vice versa, for every amount of red, an equal amount of green. And so on for all the domains of nature and the universe, since, were it otherwise, as we have said, all would be chaos. But let us keep within the limits we have set.

Very well then. Here I (or anyone else) might think of a jungle. Green, green and more green! Scarcely one or two little red flowers. How, then, does creation not explode before this imbalance? I think further: the sea. It is blue, ink-blue. A group of clouds comes and suddenly we have square miles upon square miles of green, just like that, all at once. Whither the red that will balance it? And there, hundreds of houses made of brown wood. Suddenly: fire! And immense red flaming tongues rise up into the sky, twinkling and shifting, which did not exist a second before. Where do greens rise up simultaneously, twinkling as well and shifting akin – since every shade of one demands the exact shade of the other – so that balance can be maintained?

To these questions Rubén de Loa replied without hesitation: 'Somewhere!'

Then he added nervously (the first part he had said solemnly): 'Though we may not see them – that's another matter. But, from the moment they exist, they can never cease to exist, since if they stopped existing the sudden spark of a match would be enough for—'

'Yes!' interrupted my wife and I. 'Chaos! We know already.'

'Exactly right – chaos. So they exist, even though we don't see them, they exist. And if they exist, even though we don't see them, they must be able to be reflected in a canvas, since the art of painting knows no bounds.'

We sank back into our silent contemplation of the paintings.

In effect, there were the invisible greens.

My wife, with her great, transcendental and universalizing spirit, immediately saw, floating in our friend's paintings, all the greens that accompany, somewhere, the fiery twilights that bloody all the skies of the earth each evening. She was on the verge of ecstasy.

I, who lack such a vast spirit, remained within my own possibilities. I saw only some small, fleeting greens, will-o'-the-wisps that mischievously wander the streets of this city and all cities. I will try to explain them.

Like most of my fellow men, I enjoy walking in the mornings, a little before lunch, along our beautiful Avenue Benedict XX. And like so many of my fellow citizens, many of the city's fairer denizens also enjoy walking at that same hour along that same avenue. And some of these latter like to dress in red. Generally speaking, these in particular are slender, tall and graceful; they smile, they lower their lashes, their chests swell as they breathe. I look at them then, I follow them with my gaze, I watch as they disappear around corners or into crowds, and I delight in those magnificent forms drenched in red. And I feel, why deny it, a marked unease.

For a long time, I searched for the cause of my unease, but did not find it. I wasn't content to attribute it exclusively to sexuality. There was something more, which at last, yesterday in my friend's studio, I found.

I had directly perceived those reds, sexual and burning, among the rest, because they held within them the shapes of tender young women. And yet I had no perception of the corresponding greens that would calm them, that would place them within a placid equilibrium. That was it. And because of that, when I saw them disappear, I would feel myself start to come unbalanced and plummet towards the inferno.

Never again! As of yesterday, I can walk serenely along Avenue Benedict XX. I can do so because, as of yesterday, thanks to Rubén de Loa's paintings, I have etched into my being the awareness of those fleeting green will-o'-the-wisps, invisible but out there somewhere, that trail behind every young lady who disappears from my sight shimmying in a small trickle of blood.

I turned back to Rubén de Loa.

'You have enormous talent,' I told him.

'You think so?' he asked, intrigued.

'Certainly, my friend! It's a magnificent thing to have painted the invisible greens that accompany those reds that roam seemingly alone through the world.'

And I turned back to the canvases.

Upon turning, I almost fell to my knees. There was a green there that I had forgotten, completely forgotten, and that now, as I looked anew and afresh at the canvases, appeared to me all of a sudden. Lucrecia's green, the green of beautiful Lucrecia! There it was, there it lived. That lazy green of dawn, when her body lying in bed took on a greenish hue, mouldy from so much love!

I sat there looking for a long time.

Then the green of Lucrecia, beautiful Lucrecia, began to waver, to adjourn bit by bit, so very bit by bit that I barely thought I heard a far-off peal of bells born in the convent of Los Jerónimos.

I pricked up my ears. Perhaps indeed – I don't know – Los Jerónimos were ringing. In any case, Lucrecia's body oscillated, waned.

I waited.

Lucrecia's body withdrew in its green. And in its place the greens of the friars who rang the bells began to fade, and the long greens of the tower that sheltered them, those of the stone walls that held them up, and the greens given off by their metal, clanging through the air as the friars, cord in hand, swung the clapper against it.

And this, I believe, is sufficient to pay the respect that my friend deserves. It is enough, certainly, in regard to the greens, but in Rubén de Loa's canvases there was something more: in each canvas there was a red, just one.

Anyone familiar with the theories the painter held regarding complements will understand that every one of those reds was the exact – meticulously exact, exacerbatedly exact – complement of its group of greens. As such, it is not worth dwelling on the point. Let it be known, quite simply, that otherwise, none of the aforementioned greens could have appeared, because of, in sum, that theory that leads us out into the universe itself. I will only say, to aid in better understanding the canvases, that each red leaned, according to necessity, towards a blackish maroon on one hand, towards a garish vermilion on the other; it surrendered submissively, faithfully, with such great love for the multitude of greens that surrounded it that even its very shape took part in that perfect bipolarity. At times the red was long and sinuous, coiled like a snake; at others, it was a dismembered blotch; others, a little point of spicy red pepper; others, the beautiful branches of an advanced cancer; in sum – perfection, goddammit!

And so, facing such perfection, a doubt suddenly took hold of me. I scratched my head and furrowed my brow. I lit a cigarette.

'My friend,' I said. 'This is bad.'

The man was left open-mouthed.

'Easy, my friend,' I continued. 'Let me explain. I should say, more accurately, this *could* go badly. I have just noticed – I don't know how, just like that, suddenly – that each one of the reds and all of them together do not just complement the greens of their respective canvases, but they have a much greater role.'

'Even better!'

'Listen to me. The greens of your canvases are the greens of your studio, of their atmosphere, of this vast void where you live and work. As a result, the reds that complement the greens complement not only said greens, but also your entire studio. Those reds are not only for your paintings; they are for this whole environment.'

'Even better!'

'Yes, better, as long as everyone, men and canvases, stay here inside. But what happens if you take your canvases and go out into the street, to a gallery show, for example?'

'Yes?'

'Rubén de Loa, beware, beware! If you take your paintings out of here a large part of the reds will have nothing more to do: they will lose their objective, as the environment surrounding them will be changed. Then, lacking most of the scaffolding that holds them up, that keeps them stuck and fixed there on the canvas, they will come loose, they will fall to the earth and spatter onto your shoes. And that would not be good, Rubén de Loa. Believe me, for the love of God!'

He was silent, meditating. Then he said: 'There is no danger. I've tested them and they don't fall. I've carried them out to the patio there, I've taken them to the door, I've aired them a while in the very street itself, and they don't fall. I've done even more: I've taken the twelve canvases to the apartment of the old woman next door and, one by one, I've put them in front of the multicoloured toucan. Not even its lack of green feathers, nor indeed its scarlet feathers, have managed to make the reds waver in the least bit. I repeat: there is no danger.'

'If the experiment has been done, there's nothing more to discuss. They don't fall, we agree. But that does not mean that part of the reds, when the canvases are taken out of this place, aren't left idle. You will say a small part; I, a large one. Whatever the case, we agree on the existence of this part. And this idle part, when the canvases are hung on a gallery wall, will start to seek an objective, to loiter about, to try to find a use for itself, to mortify whatever eyes may alight on it, to create fault, to sow misunderstanding, to unfurl a veil of disquiet between the viewers and the twelve canvases. And the result will be, my good friend, that no one will understand a word and everyone will leave the place with a cumbersome feeling of senselessness.'

Here I noticed that Rubén de Loa was staring at me and his face was slightly altered. I fell silent. Then he asked me: 'And? What?'

'Nothing, man! Just that. The viewers will leave with that senselessness in their pupils. Nothing more.'

'What viewers?'

'Man! The ones at the show, the hypothetical exhibition.'

He raised his gaze almost threateningly and he asked once again: 'What viewers? Answer me!'

I began to feel a certain unease.

'The hypothetical viewers of a hypothetical showing of your paintings. A thing of little importance, moreover. Why are you getting so upset?'

'Because you won't answer with the exact word. For the third time, what viewers?'

My uneasiness began to turn to fear. Rubén de Loa was getting very agitated. His eyes flashed lightning.

'The exact word?' I asked in turn. 'My dear friend, I don't know it. If not viewers, let us say aficionados or critics or simply men off the street.'

'Fine,' he said, and threw himself onto a chair. Three drops of sweat appeared on his forehead. 'Fine. Since you won't say it, the exact word, I'll say it myself. You mean to say that, leaving the gallery with eyes popping out from senselessness, will be… do you know who?'

I waited.

Rubén de Loa exclaimed: 'The bourgeoisie!'

A long silence.

Finally I said in a low voice: 'All right. Good for the bourgeoisie.'

'But, do you think,' he continued, 'that there has yet been born a bourgeois man who can manage to faze *me*? Listen well, nail it to your head if you have to, nail it on so that no pliers in the world could prise it off: if those bourgeois show up and get confused by the errant reds of my paintings, if they show up, I repeat… well, look over there!'

Fearfully, I turned to look at the corner where his index finger was pointing. My wife did the same. And we both turned pale.

There, in said corner, hung an enormous butcher's knife.

'Understand?' my friend asked. 'If they show up, one by one I will grab them by the neck with my left hand and, with that machete in the right, I'll stir their guts until they fall down dead, dead, dead! Anger? Spite? Revenge? None of those! I will crush them, grind them up, tear their insides to pieces so as to extract and expel all the reds of their blood. Then, with those reds, I will make all that are still missing in creation, all that God has planned to make during the days yet to come, reds of fire, of ruby, of flowers and meat, of menstruation and wounds, of shames and glories. I will make them all with the bloody and macerated bellies of those men: ruby, maroon, vermilion, scarlet, purple, carmine, coral, pink, cardinal, cherry, pomegranate, lacquer, flame, amaranth, tomato, cinnamon, brick, salmon, ember, spark, fire, cooked lobsters, melted sealing wax, hot iron, revolutions, flags, arteries and innards!'

Our good friend was bellowing like a wild boar. I felt my legs giving out. My wife was one fine thread away from fainting. And nothing could keep me from thinking: 'This animal is going to go crazy and chop us up like rats.'

I threw a look at my wife that was full of questioning. My look asked: 'Are you and I, in our friend's estimation, included among the bourgeois?'

And my better half looked back at me and her look replied: 'Indeed, we may very well be included.'

Without waiting for one more drop of red, I resolutely approached Rubén de Loa. I held out both hands to him effusively and said in an emotional voice: 'My good and dear friend, it's been an utter joy to make this pleasant and interesting visit to you. As soon as life offers us another occasion, we will be delighted to repeat it. But, for now, other errands await us. My dear friend, until next time then, very soon.'

And my wife: 'Sir Rubén de Loa, it has been for me an indescribable pleasure to observe your magnificent talent and partake of your charming conversation. Until next time then, very soon.'

He replied: 'Very soon, very soon.'

And we escaped in a hurry.

Outside the studio, I said to my wife: 'My dear girl, it's good we got away. We've had quite enough of greens, of reds, of painters and aquatic environments. So hurry, then. Let's go! Let's go!'

'Yes,' she answered. 'It's been quite enough. Let's go! Let's go!'

And we headed off to the waiting room in Chasuble Square.

The following dialogue, more or less, took place between my wife and me:

ME: It strikes me that the day up to now has been quite empty.
HER: No. I've found it fairly intense.
ME: In sensations, perhaps. But what conclusions have we drawn from the day?
HER: It's true. Because after all, what conclusions *have* we drawn?
ME: Anything?
HER: Anything?
ME: Nothing.
HER: Nothing.
ME: And that's just not possible.
HER: How shall we fix it?
ME: You'll see. Let's both be quiet for a long while. You go wherever you feel like going – in your thoughts, you understand. I, meanwhile, will devote myself to making observations about all that is around us. And you will see just what kinds of things I can conclude.
HER: Agreed.

The waiting room was like every other in the whole world: dull and dusty, especially dusty. We were sitting next to the window. Outside, in Chasuble Square, the daily life of said square went on. Inside, no fewer than twenty people were waiting.

I find people and objects to be of equal interest, especially in waiting rooms, where all the people are identified with the objects because of their waiting. All the same, I started with another human being like myself: the pot-bellied man sitting across from me at the other end of the room.

Yes! Certainly, a pot-bellied man! How simple to observe him! And so I turn to him; to you, anonymous pot-bellied man. Because of the simplicity of a belly clothed in cheap fabric, a belly with short legs and shoes seeping sweat, a belly with a head, and on that head a moustache, and atop it all a bowler hat. I had just witnessed events that, quite rightly, my wife had characterized as intense: I'd seen a fellow man beheaded, heard the hymn sung by thousands of cynocephali captivated by the sun, beheld the exceptional battle between two furious creatures, then the mysteries of the reds and the greens… and yet nothing! I'd drawn no conclusions at all. This means that I am not up to such great events. But now, yes, face to face, just the pot-bellied man and me.

To observe a pot-bellied man… now I think, will it be easier? To draw a conclusion, you understand, to get something out of it. Will it be easier than observing, let's say, the separation of water from earth on the third day of Creation? Perhaps. Still, as I think back over the vast range of all my reading, as far as I can remember, I know of no man past or present who has ever drawn a conclusion from observing another man who has a pot belly. I don't even know of any who has tried, who has dared to direct his attention towards a pot-bellied man seated across from him, face to face.

You will say that literature is full, glutted with pot-bellied men, and that every one of them is trailed by a writer weaving hymns of praise or psychological dramas, anecdotes or tragedies around the pot belly of his choice. Yes, that's true. Yes, but the belly itself? The belly as absolute fact, incontrovertible, the belly as categorical imperative, where is that? I know, I know! I, too, can weave whatever story I like to go with that belly. I can talk about a grey and hurried life, the outlook of an ox who grazes on home-made rabbit stew and ruminates today over what happened yesterday, only to ruminate tomorrow over what happened today. I can say that his wife no longer loves him and that the pot-bellied man suffers in silence, for he thinks that, although in principle it is unfair, in real life it is fair for a belly like his to go unloved. And, in that case, a belly is an element of tragedy and desolation. Or I can see him as lively, mischievous, not grazing on but savouring a variety of seasoned rabbit dishes, good red and white wines that make him smack his lips. He has fat friends just like him, and his wife laughs with pleasure when another cork is popped and she loves him, she loves him. And instead of chewing over yesterday's events today – not a chance! – he pondered today's rabbit yesterday, and today he will ruminate tomorrow's lion cub. And can I not thus spend my entire life – or two lives, or more – wrapping his belly in as many existences as have ever been, of all the fat men and even the thin ones the earth's crust has ever sustained? I can do anything with my pot-bellied man over there: dream, love, swing among celestial bodies or descend, sully myself and peer into the putrefaction of tombs.

This is all well and good. Yes, but what about the pot-bellied man across from me? Him, sitting right there. Him, for the fact of being there, of being. Him, for the fact of me observing him. Where is he? It's not a matter of finding out about his real life, his ideas, his desires. That would only be a return to the same. It's not even a matter of identifying with him to the extent that one absorbs him and simul-taneously lives one's own life and his. No. This is about the fact that he is there, the fact that a pot-bellied man *is*, the fact that I exist, the fact that my will has ordered me: 'Observe him, delimit him, know him.' It's about the fact that even as I try to do so, the pot-bellied man dissolves, his contours fade and he becomes hermetically sealed to me, and I sink into the same stupor as when, some time ago on a distracted afternoon, I looked and realized that there, fixed, immobile, alone, an electrical switch was stuck to the wall. And when I wanted to be certain of its reality, the switch separated me from the world, and for a brief moment I understood no more of this life or the other.

But let's return, get back to the matter at hand. Yesterday in the waiting room I had made a promise. I had promised my wife some conclusions from my observations. And so far, nothing. The waiting room's clock ticked away lost time.

Observe, my God, observe! Let us go in order. A little calm and serenity. To be sure, I know two methods by which to observe, to become familiar with another being. They are the same ones that can be used with an object, an animal, a book or anything else. Let us say a book; it's easiest for me. First method: I open it to the first page, I read the entire thing in order and I don't stop until I come to the words 'The End'. Second method: I buy it, bring it home, look at it from above, from below, from in front, from behind. I put it on my shelf. I take it out at night and flip through it. I leave it on the table. I tell a friend about the existence of the book in my house. I tell two, three friends about it. We read a random sentence on a random page. Another says to me, reaching out his hand: 'Let me see, let me see.' He pages through it with his brow furrowed and I scrutinize his expression. This goes on for several days, weeks. No one reads it, but we live inside its atmosphere. After a month, each of us gives a lecture on the book and its author. This is the second method.

Very well, but no one can deny that the first method is the one invariably employed by ornithologists and such, and that the second one is agreeable, very agreeable indeed, to bad poets.

I become an ornithologist. I make a thorough description of the pot-bellied man from head to toe: his weight, height and social status, his past, present and plans for the future, his blood pressure, desires, sufferings, bank account and all the rest of it! I ponder. Turns out, I'm no good as an ornithologist.

I am a bad poet: I will lurk near him, we'll exchange a word or two, I'll spy on his gestures at the café, on the tram, in the street, when he is alone or with friends, with his wife, with his son, when a regiment goes marching past, when a red girl walks by and envelops him in invisible greens in the middle of Avenue Benedict XX. And I will summon up – vaguely, vaguely, there in that indeterminate region between conscious and subconscious – many vague writers from vague ages who also followed pot-bellied men and did it somewhat better than I. Thus will I learn of the fat lives of the good fat people of the great cities. And I will write.

Yes, but what about the fat man right there? The clock has once again tick-tocked the lost time. And my blessed wife, right beside me in the waiting room, waits.

Oh God, how do men of talent make their observations? In any case, let's have calm and serenity, and above all, let us take things in order.

Let us begin by delimiting the fat man: to the north, the tip of his bowler; to the south, the tips of his boots; to the east and west, the far edges of hat, ears, neck, shoulders, arms, hips, thighs, legs, feet. Everything: black. On this black: the oily blotch of his face, the white blotch of his shirt, the blotch… (this is deteriorating into ornithology, but, in sum, the pot-bellied man has been delimited). Let us observe. Let us go northwards. The hat. But the hat is not the fat man, the fat man is the fat man. And if I observe the hat, I see that its peak is not the hat; the hat is the hat. Halt! We shall go straight to the fat man: there is the fat man's face, which is not the fat man, but rather… Not this again.

An overall impression, the man overall, the sum total. The total. In colour? In shape? In volume? The true total.

All three. That is to say, the environment, the atmosphere in which the fat man lives. Yes, but from here it is but a step to a bad poet's story. What to do, dear wife of mine?

The belly! The belly on a pot-bellied man, that's the solution.

It begins at the first button of his jacket and it ends at the fifth button of his fly; in both places, it spills over slightly. Very good. But let us observe the gut. I see the waistcoat. It's natural. The belly is inside. One would have to enter through the space between two buttons, between the third and fourth, because there, thanks to the pot-bellied man's posture, the edge of the waistcoat is visibly raised. Black cloth below, black cloth above, diminished light. But the black cloth above must come to an end soon and the flash of the white lining must be clearly seen. Moving on. Here we have the edge of the lower black cloth. A jump and a hop and we're on the shirt. It occurs to me that here one breathes in a dense air and also that the respiratory movements must be felt with greater intensity: up, down, up, down. And dense air. A certain discomfort, a feeling of dizziness. Good. Now, look for a way through the shirt's opening, just as we did with the waistcoat. Done. Yes, done, just one point first: is the fat man wearing an undershirt? These days have been fairly warm in San Agustín de Tango and its environs. It isn't necessary. Although in general, people like this fat man – of his age, his volume, his class – wear undershirts all year round. It's the young people, with the rise of sports, who have done away with that article of clothing. But in my opinion, it strikes me that the fat man isn't wearing one. We are, then, on the belly itself, right there on the belly. And beside the belly button. Immense, abyssal, gloomy belly button. A crater of foul-smelling mists, it rises, falls, enlarges, contracts, rises, falls, grows large, grows contracted. And at the bottom, at the bottom… what is there at the bottom of the belly button? Now that I think about it, I have never seen it. There must be little wrinkles entwined with one another. Maybe. I'm going to have a look at it.

To have a look?

To look at it! Oh hell!

And the whole belly of the pot-bellied man? And the pot-bellied man himself?

'The pot-bellied man as absolute fact, as reality, as categorical imperative…'

And me at the bottom of the bottom of two intertwined wrinkles!

Calm and serenity are essential in these things. Let's take it part by part.

There is the belly, the whole belly, circular, circular. Good. Yes, but I'm moving my eyes in a circle. I can't penetrate. I slide, I swing. I turn, and this is atmosphere and in no way the categorical imperative made flesh. This is a beginning for a bad poet. This is impressionism, vagary. I can tell because, as I spin, I see the pot-bellied man's gold chain that crosses from side to side as if it were out of focus. To really see it, I would have to rest my eyes on it. But then the belly's edges would go out of focus. What's more, the far reaches of the chain would also be blurry. I would have to go back to moving my eyes from side to side. If I stop them, I see one link in the chain, no more.

Perhaps as I look at that one link, though I don't feel it, I am still moving my eyes. But no matter. I don't feel it and that's good enough. A link. Like all the other links. He has little imagination, my good pot-bellied man. I remember other chains, those of my uncle Diego, for example, that consisted of three kinds of links. But no matter. Here they are all the same. The same? Just a moment.

Every time I see a chain, whatever length it may be, with identical rings or links, I enlarge each one, without modifying them at all, to giant proportions. I give myself over then to watching how, little by little, as they grow, they differentiate themselves to the point that I need only glance around me to know in which of them I find myself, with more certainty than that of an experienced tourist who found himself suddenly and unknowingly in China or Andalusia, in Congo or in Scotland. Incidentally, in the chain – that of the pot-bellied man, excluding for the moment any others – all is gold and nothing else. In this world, all is earth. That on the earth there are trees and they vary, and that among the trees there are rocks and beside those, waters, etc., etc., all this I know. The gold chain, increased to planetary size, also holds anything one could want. So, then, I traverse not just five continents in the chain, but as many continents as there are links, with the enormous advantage that, in the end, instead of returning to the starting point as one does on our globe, I end up somewhere totally different, somewhere diametrically opposed, with different matter, other elements, another life, another everything: a silver penknife, for example, which is surely what hangs from the pot-bellied man's chain.

And, once there, I can enjoy the magnificent, soft, cottony spectacle – as on earth I see the sky, its clouds, suns and stars – of the fuzzy depths of a shadowy waistcoat pocket.

That's the thing: the fuzzy depths of a shadowy waist-coat pocket. That's the thing: this is where all my observations have led. And there they disappear, there they will devour one other, there they will be lain to rest.

Still, I am not discouraged. It's possible that the mistake lies quite simply in having chosen the wrong method.

I have started with the large – the belly – and fallen into the small – the pocket depths. I've tried starting with the immense, the pot-bellied man himself, and I've seen that approach, as well, is a downhill slope to the tiny. And now there I am in the extreme minuscule, at the very tip of a fuzz ball in the corner of the pot-bellied man's waistcoat pocket. I must use the opposite method and perhaps all will be resolved. From the tiny we move to the large, from the fuzz ball we grow bigger until we reach the pot-bellied man in all his majesty. Little centric ball of fuzz, fuzz universe, I see it, unique and alone, cast sinuously into space, without consistence and beyond gravity. That's how I see it, but why can I not conceive of it like that? I cannot isolate it from the tiniest of breezes blowing through the pocket in which it rests. And as I think of the fuzz, I feel, I touch the distance between it and my brain, I feel and touch the distance like a living thing, permanent, like matter joining us together, matter without size or else of a unique size, since, even if I get close enough to hit the fuzz with my head, even if I move as far away as Shanghai, the antipodal city from the pot-bellied man's fuzz, it is always the same, inalterable. In the negation of that distance, there we are: fuzz, Chile, Shanghai and I. And they float, that ball of fuzz and others that intertwine with it, forming a fuzz ball of fuzz balls that is in turn thought of by me.

But neither can I think of that on its own. I think of it, as much as it pains me, along with its location in space. Without that location it escapes me, because, let's see, where would I put it? I make the pocket disappear, then the waistcoat, the pot-bellied man, the room, the city, the earth, the constellations. Nothing left but the fuzz ball, no more than that, nothing, nothing. But then, as I think about it, I can feel myself, myself in a place and not in an utter void, because the fuzz ball is out there, and it has to be somewhere in the void and in relation to me. I place it to my left, or to my right, high above me, or far below my feet. No matter where I put it I can feel my head *being* and the ball of fuzz in relation to it. Better not to make anything disappear; things always come back to the same point. The fuzz ball exists because something exists aside from it, be it only a head that thinks of it. It exists because it lies in the depths of the pocket, because the pocket's two walls rise immensely upward, clinging to the waistcoat that imbues them with existence, the waistcoat that clings to the pot belly that makes the waistcoat exist. For what is a waistcoat without a pot belly? It is the inconceivable. And if not the pot belly, there will be something else just as worthy. A waistcoat alone, singular amid utter negation, quite exceeds us. To conceive of it, it must be, and to be, it must be in *relation* to something. Best for this something to be a pot belly, because that's what I am looking at there across from me. And so on with the same thing, the same, the same. The pot belly attached to the pot-bellied man. The pot-bellied man attached to this dusty air, attached to the walls, which are attached to the entire building. A building that can only exist because there is a place to exist, and the place exists because the earth spins right along with the sun, because the sun is in relation to the constellations, which exist because they are in relation to the cosmos, which is…

All right, dear wife of mine, a moment ago I fell into a belly button's abyss, then into the depths of a pocket and now I am lost in the absolute. I am lost, undone, I've filtered through my cranium into an infinite infinity. And the fat man, in all of this? He has slipped away, the swine. The fat man is not.

Dear wife of mine, this time I will not curse again, nor will I call for calm or serenity.

It's something else that's going on here. The fat man's pot belly is something else. In order to be aware of its presence, I must allow my eyes to glide over it without focusing. For if I focus, I fall into a funnel that grows narrower and narrower, ever thinner and tighter, while everything around me dissolves, leaving me feeling like I'm in a dizzying, murky whirlwind.

Oh, pot belly and pot-bellied man! There the two of you are, made real because I do not focus in on you, because I merely glance against you. As soon as I try to grab hold, you disappear. And I set off in pursuit of a point, just one, the end point, which always eludes me because of its size and mine. And if I could shrink enough to hunt it down, perhaps – no, surely! – we would come back to the same thing, just as there is no doubt that if I could grow larger, the whole pot-bellied man would become this last real point and thus the same thing again!

Nevertheless, the fat man is there, waiting. The saintly and patient fat man, concrete. If there is anything concrete in this world it must be a waiting fat man, with bowler hat and gold chain, in a waiting room in a city that, when it comes down to it, is pretty placid.

Yes, no doubt about it, but only as long as – and here's the thing – I live alongside him in distraction. If I want everything – especially fat men – to be concrete for me, then the only way is to remain distracted always, receiving vague perceptions from all sides, letting their confused echoes resound in me like an authoritative whole that I accept in my distraction. Otherwise, everything – especially fat men – will be abstract for me.

'My darling,' I said to my wife. 'I can give you no observations, since the fat man over there – see him? – is an abstract fat man.'

'Then observe something else.'

'And if the same thing happens?'

'Impossible,' was her reply. 'Observe the lamp up there.'

Poor little wife of mine! She still believes in the differences between fat men and ceiling lamps. One look was all it took for me to realize that the tail end of the whirlwind was there as well, waiting to suck me in and carry me into the grinding teeth of all reality.

I said to her: 'No. Lamps are also abstract unless you are content to just hang them from the ceiling, turn them on at night, turn them off when there is light and dust them from time to time; unless you are content to live all your life with a nebulous, undefined idea of lamp-reality. Because, don't you think—'

'I think you exaggerate like a fool,' was her retort.

'If I'm a fool,' I said, 'it's because every waiting room I have ever seen in my life has been unbearable.'

'Then look outside.'

And she was silent.

Outside! What a difference! It's amazing that a pane, a simple glass pane no more than six or seven millimetres thick, can separate such different worlds. Outside no one was waiting, no one was falling behind the way we were at risk of doing, the fat man and the twenty or more half-alive lumps deposited along the benches inside. Outside, everyone was hurrying. It's very true that Chasuble Square is one of the most beautiful in the city. Our cities tend to be too regular, and when it comes to the squares, that regularity is perfect. But this one, which narrows towards the right side, has a certain irregularity that, at least to me, is quite pleasant. And at that hour – the sun had set by then – it all takes on a somewhat dark, steely colour. This colour in itself certainly doesn't have anything very unusual about it, but it is just right to bring out the different oranges and reds of the many lights that illuminate the square or shine from its many windows.

There are windows of cafés, of shops and of cinemas. In the café windows, you can see the customers speaking as if on mute; in the shop windows, you can see pretty much anything (I myself, from my lookout, see rubber objects). In the cinema windows, you can see luminaries and stars made of wax. There is nothing unusual about any of them. They're all ugly, they're irritating and boring, like everything that happens from the window in. As such, the beauty of the square hangs suspended at some height, unable to put down roots. It only reaches the ground by trickling down the pillars outside the windows. But it does not trickle precisely as beauty does; rather, it trickles like a notion of mine created only to express this idea that the square is beautiful and the windows are not.

Maybe the oranges and yellows of the windows *are* beautiful against the steel colour of the square. But in that case the beauty lies in the relationship between the colours and not in the square itself. And it is absurd that, the colours being so beautiful as they interrelate, the elements that produce them are so jarring. Because Chasuble Square could be anywhere in the world, and its windows could too; the former as a treasure, the latter as a bunch of rubbish. And if the whole of it is so beautiful at that hour – so say I, though I wouldn't really give a damn if it weren't for my constant fraternizing with painters – I'd say its beauty ought to be in a museum and not in a public thoroughfare. After it's produced in said thoroughfare that first time, the painters, when they grab that beauty and transfer it into their paintings, should leave a gaping hole in its place, or whatever there is of truth in such beauty. But no. They leave it, it stays right there and one can take it in and enjoy it! It would drive the sanest man crazy.

In sum, I obeyed my saintly wife. I looked and I kept looking.

Nothing, nothing, nothing! Almost the same story as with the pot-bellied man. I could have glided along weaving as many stories as I wanted to impose on all those folk in the shops, cafés and cinemas, or as many as, through evocation and distant analogies, they might have imposed on the silly receptiveness of my sensitive artist's mind.

People went in, went out, rushed, paused, greeted each other (these, the ones who greeted each other, were the ones who most sparked a deep irritation in me), looked in the windows, took seats in the cinemas, spat, smoked.

Such material! Perfect for raising up to the heavens, to literature, a thousand magnificent constructions! And even more so with the advancing hour. Already the dark steel was melting away and the lights from the windows were resplendent embers.

And I looked, dear precious apple of my eye!

But to whom would my little story about those ladies or gentlemen matter? Moreover, are they here just so I can masturbate my brain with their suits and their skirts? I hold in my very depths the certainty that they are here for something else and, as such, that I am here for something else as well. There's no way so many people exist for my own personal use and to tickle my wife's sensibility. Impossible. It would be an abracadabrical breach of logic. Or maybe they are, maybe that *is* why they're here. God knows! Because if not, what are they for? So many people! What for?

I believe that half of them could be eliminated with impunity. Kill one of every two, or even two of every three, or three of every four. Ultimately, what would change? If things – all this, the universe, the cosmos – are recorded by one gentleman or two, or by a thousand or by millions, what does that matter to things themselves? They will be recorded – well or badly, a little or a lot, but that's a different matter. If I had watched the Battle of Jutland alone, completely alone, the battle would have been the same. And the same as well if I had been with my wife, or even with my wife and the pot-bellied man and Rubén de Loa and the deceased Malleco and my brother Pedro and the consul of Uruguay and however many other people. So why not get rid of them all?

'Oh, no!' many will exclaim. 'They have to be there, even if not in Chasuble Square, so they can record, record, so their internal antennae can catch precisely the echo of the cosmos.'

What a joke! So, my dear many, I could not have stayed far away during the Battle of Jutland. Why? Because I was recording: with my eardrums, the thundering of the *Lion* and the *Lützow*; with my eyes, the flaming explosions; and with my antennae, a concept of battle. And recording it all for what? To take my concept of battle home with me, to eat heartily, make love and snore. Just like all those ladies and gentlemen out there. They're something to see! Forever recording the Total Cosmos, then going home and kicking off their shoes!

Easy now. There must be a better reason.

The reason must be there in the shop windows. Those windows and those people together make a single thing.

To the point where I cannot conceive, even with my eyes closed, of shop windows without people, or, especially, of people without shop windows.

People exist to go into shop windows. And, once they are in, to consume films, drinks and various objects, especially ones made of rubber. If shop windows were eradicated, all of humanity would scatter to the four cardinal points, and sink quickly into the oceans and slowly into the sands of the deserts. Then, in the forests, prairies and cities, the birds would intone our songs.

I would like to be the one entrusted with turning out all the lights in the shop windows. I would have the switch installed at the top of the highest tower – the tower on City Hall, for example. I would flip it with my little finger and enjoy the splendid spectacle of humanity scattering. Imagining such a spectacle calls to mind the one we witnessed at the zoo from the top of the elm tree, when men, women, children, old people, soldiers and priests went running like mad. But that time there must have been no more than a hundred thousand humans who scattered; now it would be all the billions who populate the earth. That time, they ran as fast as their legs could carry them; now they would scatter with a desperate slowness, nodding and complaining among themselves like hippopotamuses, barely, barely remembering that something had been taken from them, unable to remember and give shape to a phrase crumpled at the bottom of their memories: the phrase 'shop window'.

Of course, there will be more than a few gentlemen prone to reflection who will say to me: 'Sir, it's not the men who exist for the windows, but the windows that exist for the men.'

What can I say to that? Gentlemen's conclusions have this peculiarity: though they convince no one, they cannot be refuted.

I shall not refute, then, but: 'Sir, I still maintain the opposite. Sir, listen well. I have not the slightest doubt that if in some abandoned and inaccessible place, say the very top of Tupungato Mountain, we put a café, a shop and a cinema, soon, very soon, before you think it possible, men would start to appear from between the crags and from beneath the eternal snows. Let us now do the opposite, sir. Let us put on the top of Tupungato as many men as you like, but without shops or cafés or cinemas. They would first go mad and then they would die.'

In the beginning God created cafés, shops and cinemas. And then cafés, shops and cinemas created men. They created them when God's own initial momentum began to subside and they had to find sustenance by their own means. God, seeing this, was happy. Then came an idea worthy of Satan: 'And if we remove the fed and leave only the fodder?'

And he hid the cafés, shops and cinemas under the folds of his celestial cloak; he took them to heaven and stashed them away. And men, now aimless, with no reason for living, sprouted fur, climbed the trees and howled.

Seeing this, God, who is infinitely inclined to compassion, began, one by one, to toss down a little café here and there, and he waited. Then, a shop or two. Finally, a cinema, a cinema of sorts. And he watched. Then more cinemas, and more. And everything once again ran as if on rails. It is logical, my dear sir. Just look at our beautiful wheat fields, our beautiful alfalfa fields – exactly why are they so beautiful? Listen here, sir: it's because men and horses consume them. Get rid of these and the weeds will do away with the fields of wheat and alfalfa. Yes, my dear sir, it's like that.

The only sad part of all this, the only disheartening thing, sir – and on this we will agree – is that, be all this as it may, whether you are right or I am, whether neither of us is right or we both are, all these people will continue rushing about between the flames of the shop windows. They will go on, no matter how much leaden dust falls on me here in the waiting room. The only thing that consoles me and allows me to look upon so many rushing beings without too much envy is knowing that, no matter how much they hurry, they will unfailingly have to go back to their houses and eat. What? Some will eat in the restaurant? What a joke! And after? I ask just that, nothing more: and after? Back to their houses! What? Some will spend the night away from home? What a joke! They will go back, they will go back some day to change clothes.

Yes, but again the sad thing: no matter what, though they go to their houses and change their clothes, they will return to Chasuble Square to rush about in spite of my rage and the dust that covers me.

In short: it's no use! Here in the square it's the same nonsense as with the pot-bellied man or the lamp! Although I observe, my dear little wife, it's all the same. And if it's I who observe, or the ornithologist, or the weavings of the bad poet: it's no use, darling!

'Darling,' I murmured, 'I'm exhausted. I think I've had enough already, enough of pot-bellied men, lamps, squares, chasubles, people, cosmoses and shop windows. And so, for pity's sake, let's go, let's go!'

'Yes,' she answered, 'for pity's sake, let's go!'

Far away now from Chasuble Square, I said to her: 'I'm sorry I still can't give you any observations and haven't reached any conclusions. On the other hand, for some time now I've been observing something else, something I find to be consistently true. It is this: whenever I am ruled by pessimistic ideas, any time I want to exterminate four out of every five of my fellow men, it is because, without feeling it, I'm hungry.'

'I'm hungry and I feel it,' she replied.

We returned to the Basilica restaurant. We sat at a different table. The one we had at lunch was taken.

My wife ordered:

> Assorted charcuterie.
> *Caldo de gallo*.
> Bull testicle canapés.
> Cherimoya fruit with orange juice.

I ordered:

> Chicken salad.
> *Valdiviano* soup.

Chilean-style *charquicán* stew.
Crêpes with honey.

And for the second time that day, we both coincided on a coffee.

'Shall we go?' she asked me.

'Let's go,' I answered.

'I should like to see my family,' I said as we were leaving.

'A commendable desire,' she replied.

My family owns a kind of small mansion at the end of Sacred Heart Street. We headed in that direction. Twenty minutes later, a servant was letting us in and announcing us in the salon.

My father, my mother, my brother Pedro, my sister María and the Uruguayan consul were all gathered in the room.

From the moment we crossed the threshold, our presence seemed to inspire a frank hilarity in all of them, which they tried to suppress but which, in spite of their efforts, slipped out through the corners of their mouths.

My father is an extremely serious man. When he does laugh it becomes a national holiday in our house and the telephone is tasked with communicating the event to our whole tribe of relatives. Well, he came towards me now, smiling with his eyes, and he clapped me on the back with such gaiety that a peal of laughter burst from him like a rocket.

My mother is normal. She smiles when one should smile and laughs when one should laugh. On this occasion she showed, most intensely and with real satisfaction, a word-less approval of the general glee.

And there was my brother Pedro, over in a corner of the room, arms crossed and laughing to himself so snidely that it recalled his meanest, most unbearable moments.

My sister María barely contained herself for a few seconds before exploding into an endless fit of laughter.

And, finally, the Uruguayan consul let just a tiny bit of malice trickle out and down his beard.

Faced with this scene, I was stupefied. But all I could do was push the stupefaction back down into my body and take a seat in a chair. Then the conversation began to unfold normally, except for the intermittent eruption of ill-stifled laughter. I gradually became aware that what they were really doing among themselves was asking and answering a question during the gaps in the conversation, and although it was impossible to know what the hell it was all about, I could sum up question and answer thus: 'Is it time yet?' 'Easy, not yet.'

This absurd situation had gone on for three quarters of an hour when I realized that, to the same unchanged question, a different answer was being given. Into the air, filtered into the spaces in the conversation, was the answer: 'It is time.'

Of course it was my overgrown brother Pedro – who else? – who took the honour for himself. He came out from his corner, planted himself in the middle of the room and, looking at me slyly, spoke to me deliberately.

'Brother' – why does he always have to call me brother? Why not just Juan? – 'you pass yourself off as brave' –

everyone murmured 'Mmm' as a sign of approval – 'going at any time, day or night, anywhere in the city or outside it. But even you, brother, my valiant brother, will not dare, I bet you, do what I am going to ask you to do.'

When Pedro finished this sentence, the room was filled with a crackle of laughter. My father gave a long 'Shhhh!' and the Uruguayan consul raised his hand to ask for silence.

Pedro continued, once he had managed to calm his laughter: 'You will not dare, though it is nothing super-human – not even heroic, or even risky – that we will ask of you. We are going to ask you to… Can you guess what?'

And here, all of them – again! – exploded in irrepress-ible peals of laughter.

'Can you guess?' they asked, now more crying than laughing. 'Can you guess?'

Finally, they managed to calm themselves. And Pedro spoke once more: 'Listen, brother. The Uruguayan consul and Dad are sure your answer will be yes. Mum, María and I are betting on no. They, then, say you will dare; we, that you will not. Now it falls to you to let us know who is in the right and who is wrong. Agreed?'

I made a slight movement of my head.

'Bravo!' shouted Pedro. 'He agrees! Onward then, brother, on to the heart of the matter. I'm capable of bet-ting all my money… what do I mean, capable! I want to double my money, and I *will* bet all of it. I'm capable of that and much more, because certainty is certainty. My dear beloved brother will not dare!'

And here the dumb fool slapped me on the back.

Dad interrupted: 'My son,' he said to Pedro. 'You are, I think without meaning to, son, working in your own favour. You're dragging this out and saying too much. Let's get on with it and we will see, son.'

'Here's to Dad!' Pedro cried. Then he addressed me: 'Ready, little brother?'

I made a gesture that meant: 'I don't know, but if you want, go right ahead.'

Then everyone exploded in the most tremendous of guffaws, except for the consul of Uruguay, who politely swallowed half of his laughter and just let the other half trickle maliciously out through his beard.

They laughed like that for seven minutes. Then Pedro said: 'OK, ladies and gentlemen, the moment has arrived. Silence and… to the heart of the matter!'

'Yes, to the heart of the matter!'

'Brother, here is the bet, and we will see if Dad and the good consul are right, or if it is I, Mum and María who are. The bet is the following, which, for what it's worth, we have discussed almost all through dinner. You will see…'

'You're still stalling, son,' Dad spoke up. 'You keep manoeuvring things in your own favour.'

'No, Dad, don't you believe it. I don't need to manoeuvre in my favour, because I've already won the bet. You and the consul should be the ones manoeuvring. But, in the end, this isn't about machinations. It's about testing my little brother's bravery. Ready, little brother?'

I repeated my previous gesture.

Pedro, then: 'What do you want to bet?'

I didn't answer.

'He shouldn't bet! He can't bet!' everyone shouted.

'OK, he can't bet. Brother, this concerns the following: Dad and the good consul are sure that you will dare, and we are sure that you will *not* dare, to cross the room and look at what is behind that sofa in the corner. That's it! Nothing more. Now, let's see…'

And then came profound silence.

I was overcome. Stupefied. That was it? Over such an insignificant thing, such laughter, such betting? To look behind a sofa in the corner. Or were they pulling my leg?

My first impulse was to run and peer over the back of the sofa, but faced with the disproportion between what they were asking and what I had expected, I stopped and looked at them all in surprise.

'Well then? Are you going or not?' asked Pedro.

And again, the laughter began to splutter in the room.

'Of course he will go!' Dad said, cackling.

'And you, Mum,' asked María. 'Do you think he will go?'

'Me?' asked Mum.

And they both split their sides laughing.

'Will you go or not, for God's sake?' Pedro asked again.

Without answering, I sank into a deep meditation.

Clearly, something was there behind the sofa in the corner. Looking at it would have to produce a given effect, surely a singular one. Otherwise, there would be no reason for all the laughter. But what effect? Perhaps a horrible one? Not possible. That swine Pedro could very well have put something there that would throw me into paroxysms of horror, and he would have enjoyed it, but Dad and Mum, I'm sure, would never have allowed such a thing. I tried to imagine something of boundless repugnance. If the thing was repugnant… Let's see. I took a deep breath. All repugnant things have a foul smell. Nothing. I perceived no odour save for a trace of Vuelta Abajo tobacco leaf and that could have several explanations; there was no reason to ascribe it to anything behind the sofa. I pricked up my ears. Repugnant things teem and that teeming makes a whispering sound. Again, nothing. I barely made out a few distant little bumps, which could well have come from a small spider at work. Could it be something extremely dangerous? Scarcely did this idea cross my mind than I discarded it. If it were dangerous, fear would have taken hold of everyone there, since I couldn't think, though the world may turn in a thousand directions, of anything that would be dangerous to me and not to others. If the thing was going to lunge for my throat, it would already have lunged at María's to guzzle her young blood. If it would go after my testicles, the consul would already have lost his. I didn't doubt this for even an instant, not for a fraction of an instant. And so it was that fear never once entered my heart last night. Obviously, I felt a certain disquiet, a vague desire for someone to grant me permission to wash my hands of whatever was hidden in that corner, to break this thread uniting us, this thread with me at one end and something for me at the other, something that was becoming more and more mine, something almost me but in a different form. A single word exploded, alone, isolated, in my head: 'Jelly!' I understood. That thing must be gelatinous. It must be – if there is logic in this world – my counterpart fixed in gelatin. I have an innate disgust for all things gelatinous, above all if they are of the colour commonly known as burgundy. I'm sure I don't need to add that if the thing is of that colour and also has legs, then my repulsion is complete and, as such, unbearable. It could very well be that no such thing was behind the sofa, but it also could very well be that it was. In any case, no matter how much I thought about it, I could find no definitive argument proving it was impossible for there to be something gelatinous, burgundy-coloured and well supplied with legs behind that sofa. Well now, from the moment that a possibility exists that such a thing could be found there – I repeat, even if only a single chance – it is, any way you slice it, more prudent not to look. Certainly, deep down, I would rather have proved my father and the consul right than my rascal of a brother, but in trying to avoid three or four wisecracks from him, I could very well be exposing myself to even worse consequences. Naturally he would call me weak, a coward, a scaredy-cat, yellow-bellied, chicken-livered and what have you. Let him, that's his problem! None of those names could hurt me in the slightest because I knew, knew full well, that fear would not have the slightest influence on my decision not to look. And anyway, my wife would believe me, and if she knew and I knew then I didn't give a damn about anyone else. But here I repeat it for the record: there was no fear at all. It was something else, something that, if you like, has some resemblance to fear, but wasn't – no, it wasn't – fear itself. Because we can be specific, starting with this: 'Anxious disruption of one's state of mind because of a real or imagined danger.'

Zero right in on that bit about 'danger'! Whether it be real or imagined is another thing. Real or imagined, the danger exists. Danger is inherent in fear. One does not exist without the other, even if it is imaginary. It doesn't matter.

Well then, sirs, last night there was no danger to me at all. Never did the apprehension that I might run the slightest risk whisper in my ears. Never, never. And it seems to me that no one could doubt this, for the very simple reason that there was no danger.

No, there was something else. I don't well know how to define it, but it seems to me something like, let's say, the fear of being afraid. And perhaps even better put, fear of finding myself swept up by a succession of states of mind that, starting with my first impression at the sight of the gelatinous thing and then snowballing, growing by its own momentum, might land me right smack in the madhouse.

You will say that everywhere in the world this is referred to as fear, and the danger necessary to produce it is the madhouse in question. Let's take this step by step.

I was the first to admit that this phenomenon bore some resemblance to fear, but while resembling it, it also differentiated itself quite clearly from it, at least from fear as I understand it. It would have been fear if I had felt afraid of the thing itself behind the sofa and this – I tire of repeating – I did not and could not feel. Rather, what I feared was not the thing; it was myself once I was confronted with the thing and the successive states of mind that would ensue.

I now remember an anecdote that will shed some light on what I'm saying. Not long ago, right here in San Agustín de Tango, a friend of mine proposed a bet: a hundred pesos that I would not dare spend an entire night alone in the Catholic Cemetery. I turned down the bet. Now, anything, anyone, can intimidate me more than the dead can. A rat, an inkwell, if you like. But the dead? Why be afraid? I consider fear of the dead as absurd as fear of the number 13, or of walking under a ladder. It's something that doesn't fit with me, something I haven't got in me. But I turned that bet down flat, even knowing the other man would subject me to the same lovely words that Pedro was already preparing to hurl my way. But – and this is what I must repeat ad nauseam – it is one thing to say that the dead can do nothing to me, directly, personally; it's another thing, a very different thing, to say that I can do nothing to myself at night, when I am surrounded by the dead. I know, I know perfectly well, what I am in relation to myself as I walk along these streets, as I stroll through fields, or attend theatres and cinemas, but what will become of that relationship once I find myself alone, standing in the middle of a cemetery in the dark? All I know about that is the endless number of arguments with which they will try to ridicule me. For example, here's one: 'Sir, from the moment you know, or you feel... no, to hell with that, you *know* that the dead can do nothing against you, so why fear your own self when faced with the dead? Why not be equally afraid when faced with that chair or that hat?'

I would like to begin by saying that no one should believe I have it entirely together when faced with a chair or a hat. Naturally, the danger in this case becomes so remote that it might as well be called non-existent, but in theory – yes, that's the phrase, in theory – it is not impossible that an ordinary man, as I am, could lose his sanity when facing down a chair or a hat.

But let's finish the cemetery story; that will clear up the rest of it.

Let us look at the facts, the facts as they could have been. I'm alone, at night, in the cemetery. I am, then, in a situation entirely unknown in my life. For in my life, whenever I am alone, it is not in a cemetery and certainly not at night; when I am in a cemetery, it is not at night and I am never completely alone. So, a situation well outside my regular habits, well beyond all that is and has been habitual for me. In such a situation, it is only logical that my sensibility, my nerves, would start to try and tune into wavelengths that fit with said situation – that is, wavelengths beyond or different from everything that is habitual for me. In short, there I am, standing all alone, in the dark, smack bang in the middle of a cemetery, with graves and more graves surrounding me, at the very moment when I should be between sheets, peacefully reading with my wife beside me, hearing the habitual sounds of the city and cosily finishing off a cigarette and my book. The thinking, conscious part of me would irrefutably start to say: 'What a stupid thing I've gone and done!' And once this was said, it would naturally add: 'I shouldn't have done this. This should not be.' So then, the thinking part of me is already attached to the conviction and certainty that this is the opposite of what should be. And I will say no more about this part. To the other!

My unconscious part – my nerves and antennae that are beyond my control, the ones that send me only foggy,

99

disguised messages that I assimilate without deciphering – this part, faced with that unusual environment, would ask: 'What is all this?' And it would grow sharper, alert to the point of stridency, in order to perceive more subtle signals, ever more subtle, as it searched for an explanation.

And my components, so to speak, would be thus during the first few hours. They would give me a state of mind more or less like this: my thinking part, disapproving and unhappy as it was, would be weakened, would be less capable of rising to my defence, and the other, unthinking part, growing sharper, would gain strength and take control, it would be more ready to perceive and pick up any unusual vibrations. The part that governs me in regular life would fall silent, depleted; the part that in regular life is silent, keeping to its rightful place, would be amplified, sensitive to whatever occurred beyond the routine passing of days. In sum: me, one side regretful, the other mistrustful and alert.

I could spend the entire night that way. Dawn would come and then I would have a hundred pesos in my wallet. I don't doubt that.

But, and there's a but, if under such circumstances in the cemetery there were to occur, outside of me, in reality, yes, in 'external' reality, a sudden and unexpected event, like, for example, a gust of wind that lifted and blew a newspaper page against me, or maybe a rabbit that – zoom! – rushed between my feet, what would happen? That is what I wonder: what would happen?

Undoubtedly my thinking part, displeased and drowsy as it was, would be slow to respond, to wake up, to recover control and impose rational explanations like: it's a newspaper, it's a rabbit. My other part, meanwhile, being at the peak of its sensitivity, would begin to vibrate quickly in reaction to the event, aching to reveal itself. And with this increased disparity between the two of them, as my unconsciousness grew, grew disproportionately – now stoked by reality itself – and my consciousness floundered, beaten down by its counterpart and by its own inability to send its message of 'paper–rabbit' reality, then my animal instinct, restrained in the sun-drenched streets but now untethered, would show itself and a scream of calamity would escape my throat.

One hears one's own screams and hears their echo as well.

With my thinking part disarmed, my unconscious in charge and my instincts let loose, a scream would reach my ears – not my own scream, but a scream of night among the graves.

On instinct I would awaken and my instincts, thus spurred by the scream of terror, could perceive only one existing reality – the scream – and thus my legs would be triggered.

Run, run! Run, scream!

Run for having screamed; now scream because of the fact of running.

Because in my thoughts, in what remained of them, my reasoning could be none other, nothing more: 'I am running, this is true. From the moment I started running, there must have been a reason to run.'

And what reason is there for a man to run like that, terrified in the middle of the night? Only danger, imminent danger, deadly and ruthless. Faced with this, there's no stopping another scream. And then the whole thing repeats.

I would hear the scream again and, as it assailed my eardrums, it would confirm my terror in the face of the danger, and, on confirming it, my legs would redouble their speed. And this redoubling would confirm. And this confirmation would scream.

Run! Scream!

Until the last light of reason was completely extinguished. I still see many people sceptical about what is, for me, a well-nigh inevitable point. They will ask me: 'Terror? Horror? Of what? All the foregoing could happen, certainly, but first it is indispensable that there be a primary cause. Here it can be none other than fear of the dead. All that stuff about finding yourself in an unusual situation is not enough. And you have assured us that you could be afraid of anything *except* the dead. And so, from where is this fear born? Fear of what?'

I would answer with a question: how should I know? Agreed, I have related 'how' things would happen, but I haven't said a word about 'why' they would happen so. But how should I know that? To know that would be to know myself entirely, all my constituent parts and all the affinities these parts might have. And this is among the most absolute of impossibilities, at least as long as I am, as long as we all are, in this phase that we call man. If I knew my unconsciousness, it would no longer be unconscious. If I knew my instincts, the same would be true. And can we conceive of a man who has no unconsciousness and is beyond all instinct? Even if we can conceive of him, well,

I confess that is not what I am doing, and as for me *being* that man, it does not bear mentioning, or even insinuating. I hardly know what rolls about in my conscious mind. Hardly, hardly. And, as I've said already, I know it only on the condition that I pass alongside such knowledge, distracted, merely grazing against it, content to carry within me my whole life long a nebulous, undefined idea of everything I have seen fit to call reality.

And so, when the friend in question offered me the hundred-peso bet, I knew instantly that once I was alone, face to face with myself among those who have gone, I knew I would feel the enormous inconceivable part of me break free of the fetters that, for better or worse, are bound by this other part that I am when I think. And, once free, I don't doubt it would try to negotiate alliances that would permanently cement its freedom.

I knew, moreover, that something very small – a newspaper, a rabbit – would be all it took for that alliance to be negotiated and sealed. For if events aligned, well, we've seen the start of the fatal snowball crescendo; that is to say, my perdition.

'What a strange phenomenon!' will be the contention now.

Strange? Maybe so, if one judges by how often it happens, which is relatively rarely. But to this I say the same thing again: faced with the possibility of there being something gelatinous, with legs, behind the sofa, there being no irrefutable proof that makes the presence of such a thing in such a place impossible, then that thing *could* be found there, even if the probability is a hundred to one, a thousand to one, a million to one, or more. I don't care.

The only thing I deduce is that the possibility exists and that's enough for me. And nor is there irrefutable proof that that probability of one will not materialize in front of me.

Allow me to go further: there is, on the other hand, proof… let us not exaggerate, there are suggestions, let's say, that it *will* materialize in front of me. Why? I don't know if the answer will satisfy. It's because I felt it to be so – for me that is more than enough. Weak? No. Given that this whole succession of phenomena is, when it comes down to it, a series of internal states, I believe that the opinion of the person who is going to experience them is quite worthwhile, for the very simple reason that he is already part of the ensuing succession of phenomena.

But let us leave aside whether this might happen one time in ten or once in a million. Let us leave aside whether, when it happens, it is to me or to someone else. There is something else that I want to say to those who would argue the impossibility or even the strangeness of such a thing.

Sirs, I would say to them, this happens every day, at all hours, to all men, no matter how serene and worthy they might be. It happens, and I'm going to tell you how. That it does not reach its culmination is another thing, the thing of one in ten, one in a million. This, as I have said, I have left aside.

A good gentleman – the pot-bellied man from the waiting room, for example – goes out for a leisurely stroll. He has all his constituent parts in perfect balance. The conscious part mildly and distractedly registers the things that, as he walks, his senses take in. His eyes say: 'How prettily the sun is shining!' An echo, his consciousness responds: 'How prettily the sun is shining!' The ears say: 'That song is from a thrush, and that, no doubt, is the train going by.' And the consciousness says: 'That song is from a thrush, and that, no doubt, is the train going by.' His palate says: 'Jesus, what dreadful beer!' And the confirmation comes: 'Jesus, what dreadful beer!' His feet say: 'How pleasant to walk on such soft ground.' And the echo: 'How pleasant to walk on such soft ground.' His nose says: 'It smells like cheese.' And the thinking part confirms: 'It smells like cheese.'

The unconsciousness, discouraged, dozes. Sometimes, now and then, it raises its head, startled awake by what it thinks is a possibility for action. No! False alarm! It was the smell of cheese, nothing more. It dozes off again. An *entente cordiale* is definitively reached, a cordial and moreover terribly boring understanding: the first part will be lord over all the pot-bellied man's brain and the man himself, throughout his life; the second part will be content, from behind, to give general outlines, contours of the whole, broad imperatives. The cordial understanding is sealed. The fat man continues his stroll, returns to his house and talks about the sun's rays, the thrush's song, the sip of beer, the benevolence of the pavement, the doubtful smells.

Yes, sirs! This is how fat men go for walks, and thin ones as well. But believe you me, this is not all. The other part dozes, yes, but it dozes like a guard dog. At our good man's slightest lapse, it takes advantage of the most trivial singularity in the environment and it sends him signals. Two colours, two shapes that the sun catches, jumbles, amalgamates, transforms; two that, without erasing the identities of objects, would make a painter stop, paint and think that perhaps the whole universe could have been different from how it is. Well, the fat man's unconscious also murmurs to him thusly. The fat man is alarmed. The fat man asks: 'What? What's that you say? What, what?' Then his consciousness, master of the situation, steps forward. 'Nothing, my good sir, nothing! It is straw the sun alights upon, grass that it doesn't, a brick wall that is not violet, only brick red. Those are the shapes of trees, eucalyptus – yes, my friend, eucalyptus – and walnut trees that grow walnuts, and nothing more.' The alarm passes. The fat man thinks: 'Yes, yes, yes. The owners of so much barley and alfalfa must live well. Brick will pass with the advent of cement. If I were in government, I would not let one single eucalyptus be cut down. I've never been able to swallow walnuts; I prefer almonds.'

And he continues his stroll. The whole thing has occurred with only a slight wrinkling of his brow or a brief hesitation in his step. The fat man continues on and he will drive his cane into the ground with a thump, just one, more forceful than those that went before. He continues. He has left the painter behind, frozen, blocked. He has left him tangled up in the same questions, but asking, begging that they be asked again and for a long while. 'What did you say? What was that?' And there he remains, he is gone. On the fat man's way home, he buys a packet of almonds.

All of this, from murmur to forceful cane thump, has not taken more than a hundredth of a second.

Or from the cry of the thrush or whatever it may be. The man again furrows his brow. From one tip of his brain to the other have swung a thousand evocations of remote pasts. Or the soft ground. Through his shoes, a thousand unsuspected associations have clambered up, which, if they were caught and strung together, would encompass a whole chunk of the world if they were not allowed to pass. It is better that they are. Remote pasts, unsuspected associations? 'No, my friend, the birds sing and they have always sung. It is pleasant to step on the soft ground as long as it isn't too soft, for then the walk would be difficult.'

He is still the pot-bellied man. A poet would have been ensnared. The pot-bellied man returns to his house. The painter or the poet, no. But return they must, whatever the cost, and so to extricate themselves, the former makes a splotch and the latter writes a poem.

This is how it is, my dear sirs. Not just for poets and the like. For they already exist partway between the two modes. It is like this for everyone. For all of us, at any time, the calls ring out, but not everyone stops every time or pays enough attention.

For everyone, and for my pot-bellied man from the waiting room as well. It is just that, for our pot-bellied man, the time has not yet come for him to go mad.

But, let us see, sirs: have you understood by now that, faced with a chair or a hat, I don't have it entirely together?

But that's not the point. Let's see.

I was afraid, at the time of the bet, of stopping and paying enough attention.

You will refute me once again: 'Why would you start to pay enough attention there, you who ramble among all the evocations and associations of light, of musics, of all the senses, you who ramble and forge on unafraid? If you were afraid of the dead, we wouldn't argue. But, you say...'

Back to that again, my God! The fear of the dead... That's not it, my dear sirs. It's that, at a given moment, when I might be affected by a certain internal imbalance, or, if you like, by a different balance, one that is unusual for me, with the conscious guard weakened, with the demons of my unconsciousness freed, then anything, a rabbit, a newspaper, might let loose...

'Might let loose...'

That's it.

'But let what loose? You are not afraid of the dead, so your grounds are lacking, the thing to be loosed is lacking.'

My dear sirs, it's true; I am not afraid of the dead. But can I know how many fears of mine sleep nested in the unconscious depths of my being? Can I be sure they don't exist, just because, so far, I have not beheld them? I have only to go back in time a few generations to find in all of my ancestors a panicky fear of the dead. I have only to speculate about what my childhood must have been like with those old witches who took care of me, so as to leave no doubt that I personally must still have feared the dead. Where are those fears today? They must be there, sirs, they must be there. They won't surface as long as the circumstances around them are averse to the modification or deviation of my sensible thoughts. But as soon as I start seeking so recklessly to give them an opportunity, it's possible those fears will find, suddenly, exactly the opportunity they need, and then nothing can hold them back and they will overflow, because they will have found, outside, once my judicious consciousness is dozing, the means to make viable the beliefs from which they, those limitless terrors, sprang, and the beliefs become reasonable once again, and everything coincides perfectly – environment, beliefs and terrors.

Sirs, it may be that a cemetery at night is not the scenario it would take to set loose so much evil. I am still inclined to believe that it is not. If it were, you will not disagree, it would have too much of the primal about it, it would be too reasonable for our everyday reason: fear of the dead, cemetery, night, graves, solitude. I am inclined to believe that this would not be it. That's why I have often felt a distinct fear upon going to open a door or look beneath my bed. But, who knows!

The only thing I know, and know thoroughly, is that when two things – just two, no need for more – fit together exactly, with utter exactitude, and with enough power and duration, no one can foresee where it will lead.

Do you understand now, I repeat, why one cannot be too trusting when faced with a simple chair or a simple hat?

And now let us return, sirs, let us return, please, to the sofa in the corner of the living room in my parents' mansion.

No one can deny that the thing there was a bit more severe than facing hat or chair, that it was perhaps as severe as it could have been in the Catholic Cemetery. Yes, perhaps as much, for the very clear reason that my good brain could not come up with a logical explanation using the various elements to be found in that living room: the laughter, the anomaly of the proposition, that gelatinous suspicion of mine, the Uruguayan consul...

My brain was not supplying me with the necessary defences to react quickly when faced with the start of a snowballing succession of events that would become a frantic race and stop, there at the end, with a madman.

The only thing my brain had supplied me with was the idea that the thing had to be gelatinous. Yes, gelatinous. And so, last night, in the living room, I grew stronger in this conviction: behind the sofa there could be something gelatinous and, worse still, it could have legs and be burgundy-coloured.

And so I grew stronger, surer, intensely so. So much so that I almost stepped forward and looked.

But it was precisely this blind faith that impeded me from any movement. For – my salvation! – I managed to reason with myself as follows before I took the first step: 'All of my precautions have been taken assuming that the thing is gelatinous. If it is, there will be hand-to-hand battle. But if it isn't? If perhaps it is made of something that is completely the opposite, or of something that so far I have been unable to imagine?'

Sirs, in such a case, when I looked I would find myself – leaning over the sofa like that – naked, defenceless, ready to be taken prisoner by the liberated unconscious, at the mercy of all that lies within it, anaesthetized by the noise of the peoples of this city.

Prudence! Prudence! You must remember as well, dear sirs, that my existence is not entirely mine. I am married, sirs. I have responsibilities and duties to fulfil. Prudence above all!

'All right then! Are you going to look or not?' my brother asked.

I answered: 'No.'

'Eh! You plucked little bird!' he exclaimed. 'Good consul, dear Dad, you have lost.'

And everyone chuckled softly.

And then they began to speak of everyday things and to share them with us good-naturedly. But, as their voices grew louder, I drew near my wife and said quietly: 'Don't you think this is enough of foolish bets and corner sofas?'

'Enough already,' she answered.

'Then, I beg you, let's go, let's go!'

'Yes,' she repeated, 'let's go! Let's go!'

We were going down the steps of the mansion when, from above, we heard Dad's voice: 'Children! Wait a minute! I'll walk with you for a few blocks.'

We waited outside, two steps from the front door. Dad took three minutes. Before leaving, he stopped to talk with the doormen a moment. In the light from their anteroom, I could see that he had put on a bowler hat. It was the first time in his sixty-five years that I'd ever seen him in such a hat. Dad has the most complete collection of hats: three panama hats, a trilby, two black top hats and a grey one, several caps, four explorer hats, a straw hat, three berets and six nightcaps. But a bowler... never! I even thought that perhaps, in his distraction, he'd taken the consul's hat by mistake.

The moment of chatting with the doormen extended for four more minutes. Finally, we heard Dad wish them goodnight and he came towards us twirling his cane. He paused a moment on the threshold, gazing at the shadowy buildings across the street. Then he took a step forward. Just as he did, it rained.

A fine and monotonous rain. We set off into it, hunched over. I thought only of Dad's bowler hat, which would be getting wet and would, surely, be leaking. And also, in the intervals, I thought that without and beyond a doubt, San Agustín de Tango is a really stupid city.

And so I could not comprehend – the city being so markedly stupid – how a man, a patrician, a gentleman above all, could enjoy walking a bowler through its streets on a rainy night.

'Dad,' I said to him, 'why don't you go back home? In this rain you could catch a cold, or even the flu. A bowler is not enough to save you from an illness like that.'

'You must not make observations of any kind to me,' was his response, and he continued to traipse along beside us.

The ill fate of that hat oppressed my soul. I dared not look at it, but I could feel it leaking, dripping, more and more, perhaps melting very softly over Dad's bald spot, that dear bald spot I had kissed so many times. But anyway. We traipsed, the three of us traipsed, splashing one another and without looking at each other.

At a light, Dad stopped. We stopped as well.

I took the opportunity to ask a question. It was regarding a topic that had been tormenting me for some time, with which – parallel to my heart's oppression over the bowler's likely fate – I was becoming more and more obsessed as we walked.

'Dad,' I asked him, 'do you think that during the Great War, in the middle of battle, if an inhabitant of Jupiter had come down to Earth, the armies would have gone on fighting?'

'I told you I'll have no observations. And I certainly won't accept any questions.'

We were silent.

Finally, he said to us: 'Well, my children, you go on. I'm going back.'

'Bye, Dad!' we said in unison.

'Goodbye. And not another observation, not ever.'

We continued arm in arm, our hands getting wet.

I said to my wife: 'Well, now it's his own fault if the rain melts him. I don't think his outing concerns us at all any more. It was a different matter when his steps were matched with ours. But now? From the moment he turned away…'

'I'm a bit cold,' she murmured.

'That light is coming from the Barefoot Tavern.'

'Let's go there.'

'Some hot lime flower tea would do us very nicely.'

'Very nicely.'

The Barefoot Tavern is always the same. I looked with some sadness at the table where one night, perhaps a rainy night like this one, the unfortunate Malleco had sat with his friend who revealed the mysteries of love.

We ordered two lime flower teas, which we began to drink in silence.

'One moment,' I said to my wife. 'I'll be right back.'

I went down to the urinals and, with my forehead resting on my right forearm, I answered nature's call. I looked down at the five little holes drilled into the white porcelain urinal: one above, another below, one to each side and a fifth in the middle. I tried to move my stream from one to the other successively, spinning like the hands of a clock, never touching the middle hole.

Then, on my third time around, when I was on the right-hand hole and about to move to the one below, a fly suddenly landed on the edge of the same side of the bowl. One slight movement, if I was quick, would have served to annihilate it. But if I did that, the hands of the clock would not go on turning. I had, then, to choose between clock hands or fly.

One point. The decision had to be fast – instantaneous, really – because any vacillation would cause time to split into two: the march of the turning hands and the pause of indecision. And with time thus differentiated, bifurcating, its unity would be broken, with one part continuing 'to be' and the other becoming separate from it. That's to say, the other part would be outside of time.

If I had gone for the fly without hesitation, nothing essential would have come of it, since by not hesitating – that is, if there'd been no pause at all – time would have continued to be one and the same, though filled with something else: no longer holes in a urinal bowl, but rather a dying fly. And as such, in life there would only have been a change of elements, of objectives, and all would still be within a single unity, and there would have been no fundamental alteration.

Well then, I have no doubt that there was, on my part, hesitation. It must have lasted, certainly, some millionths of a second. This doesn't change the fact that the hesitation was there. It doesn't change the fact that, for a millionth of a second or however long it was, time kept going, kept being, while I hesitated before it. It doesn't change the fact that I, hesitating 'in' time, stopped being part of time, or rather – more like it! – stopped *being* time, as one surely always is. And by not being time, the conditions were apt – for a thousand millionths of a second if you like, it doesn't matter at all – for me to be hit by time and to notice it.

I have not the slightest doubt that's how things went.

An infinitesimal point, surely just as infinitesimal as the aforementioned time period, in the space between the hole on the right and the one on the bottom, was for me like a mirror that reflected time, which circulated without me. It was that solitary little point, minuscule, luminous, that came unstuck for me.

Certainly, I had the – I don't know whether to say vision or feeling, let's go with the latter – the *feeling* that the hands had continued alone on their circular march. Then, as they did this – that is, as they separated themselves from me – I had the feeling of a suspended impact.

I will explain with an example that has never happened to me, but which I have imagined a thousand times, in particular just before I fall asleep.

I am high up at the edge of a precipice. I leap from it. I fall. Unimaginable speed. But I am held at the waist by elastic. The elastic unravels at the same speed at which I'm falling and does not diminish this speed at all. But the elastic is shorter than the height of the precipice. Then comes the moment when I am brought up sharply. Leave aside the fact that the elastic, as it stretched, would gradually create more resistance. That's not how it happens in my imagination. Instead, I am brought up sharply, instantaneously, without the elastic having impeded the acceleration of my fall in the slightest. And only here, in halting my vertiginous fall, does it act like a regular elastic band. It retracts and I'm suspended.

Huuuuup!

I cannot help but write 'huuuuup'. Pardon me. I want to record the sudden feeling, somewhere between distressing and delightful, that one would experience from such a fall and such a suspension. And don't forget, all of this is happening over a precipice that's higher than the highest mountain range and at speeds that are, as I've said, unimaginable.

Well then, when playing out this image in my mind, there is another image inherent within it: although I am suspended, not everything is correspondingly suspended. Another part – the one that includes all my ideas, all my memories and experiences, my entire life, all that exists in my head, conscious and subconscious, in sum, everything – continues to fall. Only my body is suspended, along with my perceptive faculties. Then, for an instant, I see, I contemplate, I consider, there below me, scattered but still united and simultaneous, my entire past. I see it there in one single point and all at once, since I see it without the chronological succession of time. There, along with the day of my birth, is the very moment before the elastic's contraction. There, along with those two points, is all that is enclosed between them.

But then the surprised and falling part reacts as I had a moment before. An invisible elastic cord connecting it to my head stretches to its furthest length and retracts. This separate part rises upward at the same time that my own elastic, now weighted down by my body and lacking the force to contract, again stretches downward. It rises, I fall. We collide, we fit together. And chronological order again

117

stretches out, snaking among everyday complications. My birth withdraws into oblivion, the instant of collision has been just the latest occurrence in my life.

That's it.

I execute this vertiginous jump nearly every night. But, of course, in a purely imaginative way. I am not talking about the jump itself, no. Needless to say, I don't walk up to the edge of any precipice, etc. Such a thing is a given. By saying it is purely imaginary, I refer to the fact that, by mentally executing said jump, I remain, to a certain extent, separate from the man whom I make fall, in spite of the fact that said man is and can be none other than myself.

I am myself and I 'try' to imagine what I would be feeling if I fell. This 'trying' already puts me at something of a remove. Then comes the suspension, the point of culmination. Here comes the feeling of splitting in two that I've spoken of, its absolute possibility – nay, its inevitability – and with it, the distinct feeling of being in the presence of an entire past that has been freed from time and appears all together, simultaneously.

Yes, there is this feeling of the certainty of splitting, but there is not the past itself. I see nothing of the past, my birth and my childhood do not appear, nor does any hidden memory come to light. I have the feeling of its inevitable possibility, but not the phenomenon itself.

Well then, yesterday evening, in the toilets of the Barefoot Tavern, the phenomenon itself occurred, it was seen and I saw it, I felt it and entered into it through that millionth of a point in that millionth of a second.

When time went on passing, made real for me by the existence of two invisible hands, when I escaped from it with a suspended hesitation occasioned by the sudden presence of a fly, when that happened, there shone a momentary spark containing the phenomenon that, until then, I had imagined but never seen.

But it was small, very small. Nothing of births or childhoods or years or even months. It was only a day, only one: yesterday.

In that instant ground up to its minimum part, there appeared, simultaneous and interpenetrating but without the slightest confusion, all the events of the day, isolated and clear, free of any chronological order. And as they so appeared – to my astonishment, my joy, my ecstasy, my supreme delirium – I saw, I felt, I knew, finally, *life*, the truth stripped of all deceit, all sensationalism, or, better said, of everything that limits life to an unreal sequentiality.

An unreal sequentiality! Yes, that's it. I now know that's how it is.

I saw all of yesterday's events for what they were, what they are. I saw what it was that had previously made me see them as being shelled. That's it: shelled like peas into a full container. No. They had always been, they are, without that within.

But I cannot say what they are, what I saw there. Later I'll explain the reason for this forced silence, but in order to do that I must first relate how, just after that millionth of a second was past, things began to ensue again, ensuing.

On to that, then.

As I have already said, it was all joy, delirium, ecstasy. Finally, I knew. Then I was struck by the image of she who is the companion of my days, sitting beside her hot lime flower tea, and my nostrils were whipped by the scent of sleepy countryside, waiting upstairs in my own mug.

A hot lime flower tea is a very good thing. Even more so when you think that, between one sip and another, you will be revealing the Truth to Her.

I had to go up. I hurried. I don't remember at what point I stopped pissing. As for the fly, it had gone.

I arrived. My tea was steaming. My wife was staring into space. Over at the late Malleco's table, two guys were chatting and drinking rum.

Catching sight of me, my wife asked: 'What happened to you? You look like you've seen the light.'

'Just a moment, just a moment!' I answered. 'I have the key to everything. But, my darling, this is not the place for revelations of such import. Let me drink my tea first of all. Then... you will see!'

I drank calmly and with gusto. Waited a few minutes, lit a cigarette. Then I asked her: 'Don't you agree that, in view of such a revelation, we should be going? Our home is waiting. Our bed! Soft lights. Yes, my dear wife, enough of lime flower tea and taverns. On to the revelation! Let's go!'

She responded gently: 'Enough of taverns, it's true, enough of lime flower tea. The revelation is coming. So let's go!'

I rent a small apartment at 9 Altar Cité, fourth floor.

Scarcely had we arrived than I said to my wife: 'Don't you think that the centre of our home is our bed? Lying down, parallel to the earth, with soft light, what calm! When we are there, I'll reveal to you what I know.'

Once I was in bed, I called her to me and said: 'Wait for a bit in the next room. Give me a few moments to myself. Let me recall that moment to mind, clarify it, and then I'll talk to you.'

She left and I turned off the lights. Then, in my imagination, I went back to the urinal and again smacked right into the movement from the second to the third hole.

I hit against it, I bounced up, the holes swung beneath me, I swung above them, and at the first separation, *that* flew around my head, crashed into it a few times, fluttered, flew, then took off.

Just like the fly in the pisser. Yes, like the fly, it took off. Here, with some surprise, I remembered I had seen the fly fly away, I had noticed it, noticed it take off. That is to say, I had seen the following: I'd been looking at a black dot on the pristine bowl, when instantaneously a white dot fell on top of the black dot and the bowl was, with the same instantaneousness, totally limpid and above all white. That was all I saw, nothing more. Now, in terms of what I thought, that's a different matter. I thought that a fly must have taken flight when a white dot fell where the black one had been, and that, as such, my fly had to have been in the air at that moment. A turn of the eyes and I saw, in effect, the fly in question disappearing. And it all gave me a sense of great security, to have confirmed that events had taken place with an unbreakable logic of succession. The strange thing is that I felt the same way now, as I watched the revelations I'd acquired at the moment of my suspension and the bifurcation of time move off, disappear. I felt that this knowledge, like the fly, was taking off as well. Yet I wanted it to be not like one fly, but like three. With an empty brain, then, with utter inanity, I followed them all in their flights. I said to myself: one flies off down the corridor, another goes into the toilets and washes its hands, the third has gone out through an open window and is soaring over the inner courtyard. And as I had this thought, I felt myself redden a bit, embarrassed that a man could imagine his revelations as three little flies buzzing around outside of him. And most of all, I was ashamed that that man was me, none other than me.

In truth, a brain must be very empty for such thoughts to spring up in it. Can there be any doubt? For a moment I wanted to believe that, after all, it was kind of funny, this idea that such profound knowledge was transformed into three little flies, and that one of them – that is, a third of the knowledge – was in the toilets washing its hands. But that thought didn't last, it couldn't take hold for more than a second. The truth was something else: my brain was emptying out and I was headed straight for inanity. Proof? Here you go.

The entire world, the real one, had entered my room as the three bugs escaped. It was there once again, enveloping me and blending into me. I now heard all the noises around me and spontaneously located them in space: here, my breathing imitated a bellows, and the bed creaked with my body's every inattention; there, a cockroach scratched under an imperfection in the wallpaper; outside, people were talking in the inner courtyard, and their words reconstructed the entire building, lit by some windows that formed the Altar Cité that radiated streets in every direction and that issued sounds of their own; a car, a tram, the constant murmur of it all and of all the inhabitants of this city; my wife next door, her hair is brown, her eyes sleepy, the neighbouring room is perfectly square, I have two mahogany chests, Dad lives on Sacred Heart Street, I touch the sheet with my fingertips, today is about to end, the previous day is over, tomorrow will come and then another day and another and another and through all of them I will keep moving my feet so I don't fall flat on my face. I hear, I see, I feel all. There is a faint scent of camellias. I hear, I feel, I see, I live. Can there be any doubt that my brain has emptied like a communicating vessel levelling off with reality? Goodbye, public urinals! I knew that my best ideas, my vast perceptions, had always come while I was in public urinals with my forehead resting on my right forearm while I let Mother Nature flow and pass through me. Now I was in bed, only to get up the next day and return to it at night. To eat, greet, comment, dream, yawn and love and finally sleep so I can wake up and recommence, day to day, elbow to elbow, bone to bone with my fellow man, with the air, with the ground and with the act of living.

So, how did it go again? I repeat it all in vain. The five holes, the fly, etc. It's all just an episode that does not echo within me.

My wife is waiting in the next room.

Let's go in order, part by part. Let's begin, as with anything when you want to end well, at the beginning. Here goes.

The day began with the business of the guillotine.

(Here I remembered, I went over everything, all the events one by one. Before I did, I recalled the proceedings against poor Malleco. This I recalled in a block, all at once. But everything I had personally witnessed, no. Here, I repeat, I went part by part, with such faithfulness and precision that when the little groom made his final bow to us, I had to take my wife by the arm, and as I took it, the San Andrés Zoo had to appear before me and, above all, I had to hasten towards it.

After all, wasn't that what it was all about? Of course! As such, we are perfectly fine so far.)

The San Andrés Zoo. Clearly, the San Andrés Zoo.

(The fourteen she-lions filed past me, then the cyno-cephali. I looked at them one by one. One by one, so

124

closely that I saw several I hadn't noticed while I was at the zoo. I replayed the song, with all its heights and all its depths. I didn't miss a single one of my emotions. The underground waters, the knives, everything. I experienced again how the ebullient enthusiasm welling up in the souls of two humans grew bitter along with hundreds of beasts. I relived it all with such intensity and precision that in came hastening the now implacable logic of what had to come and hasten in, because it had hastened just so in reality, as I struck, flattened against and slid down the body of reality itself. Yes, yes, the rock grew dark and our voices, wounded birds, fell back down our throats. It had to be so and I, there in my bed, had to again feel the desperation of a dark cloud that swallowed up all our enchantment. I had to say 'Let's go, let's go!' and, precisely because this sound was produced and its echo resounded, a lion, close by, had to have escaped.)

The she-lion. That's it. Now comes the she-lion. Part by part we see the lioness, and then the ostrich. That's it. The ostrich, part by part as well.

(Yes indeed, part by part!) Nothing escaped me. I seized each part, I squeezed it, ground it up. And with each one I was astonished by how many more things I had observed and seen without having paid attention, without having had the slightest awareness of them. In sum, it was staggering how much I had really lived in each part, especially compared to what I have written down here. What I have here is nothing. For example, when, as the lioness finished her jump and the ostrich stepped to one side, you will remember that it called to my mind Belmonte's movement as he faced the bull, when I was at the bullfights with the beautiful Lucrecia. Well then, yesterday evening as I lay in bed, I realized that in the moment when I was with my wife high in the giant elm tree, as I remembered the bullfighter, I had actually evoked the entire bullring, and I had recalled the violent tumble of a picador confronting the same bull, and also Gallo, when he was booed for being afraid of the previous bull, and, what's more, I had heard again, with lightning speed, the voices of the newspaper vendors as they sold the morning paper with the story of the bullfights, 'Valerito and Belmonte triumph! Gallo flounders!', and the beautiful Lucrecia, just as the newsboy said *Gallo*, had lit her cigarette in the earthy darkness of our hotel room. Our hotel! Now – meaning last night in my bed, not high up in the elm; in the elm I had recalled only up to the flare of the match and no further – now in my bed I saw again, complete in all its detail, our hotel in Zaragoza, which enclosed within that earth-coloured room, and even the stairway and the water-yellowed lobby, all of Lucrecia's laziness and the tedium of seven days at the Basilica of Our Lady of the Pillar. Our Lady of the Pillar made Lucrecia languid; she yawned and stretched, lengthening and twisting her lustful urges like elastic bands. That's why the mornings in Zaragoza brought out, better than ever, the mouldy greens of her body.

The ones revealed by Rubén de Loa.

Rubén de Loa? Not yet. That's all wrong. We're missing the end of the skirmish, we're missing lunch. I've accidentally strayed to the far reaches of yesterday. Back in line, back in line!

The skirmish ended. Not allowing my thoughts even one detour, I ate lunch, tasting again every flavour of every dish. So unswerving and defined was my concentration that, stumbling through the fog, we've arrived at our friend's studio.

(It was something to see, the certainty with which I retraced the hours in the studio. I had only one slip-up, or one near slip-up. It was this: precisely when I arrived at Lucrecia's greens, they overflowed beyond the studio. There, they had been an evocation, only one – one brushstroke I would say – of all the greens of our shared life. Nothing more. On the other hand, yesterday evening, I repeat, they started to overflow: one part of the sum total of her greens had detached, and this part was, precisely, those greens from the dawns in the Zaragoza hotel. Such that, when those greens appeared to me, I couldn't keep the flare of her match from appearing as well: the newsboys, the bullring, Belmonte's step, the ostrich's step, the elm and our race towards it, the cry of terror – 'The lion!' – and even our calm walk before the fight and after the cynocephali. That is to say, one point more, and I'm taken back inexorably to waking up at dawn, the very early dawn, to attend the execution of poor Rudecindo Malleco. And once there, only God could know how far my backward march would carry me. But I sensed the danger just as I glimpsed a monkey's large head emerging, rising up like a ray of light. I made a violent effort, and with one foot in the studio's safe green and the other in the intrusive green of Zaragoza, and barely, just barely, feeling our lunch between the two of them, especially the seaweed with onion – which, I thought, could be bad for me – I made, yes, a violent effort, and I launched myself forward, head down, with such momentum that I crossed without hesitation, without distraction, without temptation, through all the reds of this world and the next, down to the very last one, and the fear of my friend's machete led us to leave that aquarium and made us say we'd had enough already of such things.

And then nothing could, nothing would, have been able to stop the waiting room with its fat man and the beautiful Chasuble Square from unfurling in my head.)

Waiting room. Chasuble Square. Here they are.

(The previous effort was fruitful. Not one deviation this time! I went back over the waiting room and the square and held fast to both, though I seized on and experienced every detail again, though I sensed that many of them were full of little escape hatches that opened onto their own far-flung, singular scenes. But no. Sure, sharp, iron-willed, I went on. At a given point, I unhesitatingly attributed the unease I felt to my empty stomach.)

The Basilica restaurant.

(A magnificent success! Because I really don't think this bit qualifies as a deviation – though, I should mention, something similar will happen again when I remember the scene in my family's house: there went the chicken salad, there went the *valdiviano* soup, the Chilean-style *charquicán* and the crêpes with honey. They went by with such veracity that I thought it exactly like a ruminating ox. I mean, I must have thought that. I don't know! Could there have been a mistake, then? All I know is that somewhere in there between the *charquicán* and the crêpe, I saw, I glimpsed, without thinking, the head of an ox with two enormous horns. That's all.)

And here we are in my family's mansion, the corner sofa, that idiot Pedro, etc. Here we are on the street with Dad and a fine rain.

(Here, as I said, just one tiny deviation, slight, slight. It was in the cemetery. Without thinking anything, absolutely anything, without straying from the course of what happened in the house, without any interruption in our travelling of that course, I saw, sudden and alone and for a brief instant, that grave with the smooth horizontal headstone and a somewhat lopsided yellowed cross, where lies, and has lain for two years now, the Polish man from the little tobacco shop next to the Legal Prison, that sly Polish man who'd sold me cigarettes so many times. That was it.)

And so, we enter the Barefoot Tavern now, order two lime flower teas, and I go downstairs to the public urinals.

(All of this was covered well. I'll say only that: well. My concentration was perfect, no distractions existed. What keeps me from being able to call this round 'Magnificently good!' is that, from the moment we crossed the threshold of the tavern, I began to feel slightly nervous when I foresaw the culminating moment drawing near; the great moment when I would again, without a hint of a doubt, see and know what I had seen and known before.)

The bowl, the five holes, the fly… the moment. GLORY!

Yes, glory. Because it came back to me. I proceeded so surely and firmly, making each particle of an instant spring up, that each one of them inevitably birthed the next. No possible force could have prevented the urine's momentary hesitation between hole and fly. All efforts were channelled and concentrated with a single-minded will that flowed towards that point and so that point exploded. And so, glory. I separated myself from time again. Glory. And to this separation the present moment was added, as well as the previous moments of climbing the stairs, drinking the tea and returning home, to bed. It was the same again, plus everything that had happened since. That is to say, the same and a tiny bit more. So, let us twice say glory. Like so: glory, glory. Very good. But here came a slight deviation: I remembered that all of this work had been aimed at again reaching 'the moment' and offering it up to my wife with both hands. And so, without a doubt, my life was now tolling the moment to seize the moment. I felt a name – her name, Isabel – nearly emerge, the groundwork laid for the uttering of a letter 'I'. But I did not call out. What silence reigned in the apartment and everywhere else! I did not call out.

With one single-minded will these efforts, channelled and concentrated, surged onward with such momentum that, no doubt about it, that will was no longer mine. Now it had become the will of the internal process I had unleashed. And oh, I want you to know that I suffered a dreadful pain here! My squalid, pale will, tearing and rending itself, wanted nothing more than to grasp those first foundations of the 'I', to form it and all the rest of the letters and then wrap itself up in them as if inside a suit of armour and wriggle free of the torrent of one whole day of life, to wake my wife with a shout and bring her here to help me hold on to that moment of utter knowledge and total sensation, so that we could build on it all that was left for us to live!

It was a pygmy's battle against a giant. Not even a battle, it never rose to that level. It was nothing. It was just a miserable invalid watching the invading army march past. There wasn't the remotest possibility of articulating that 'I'. To say nothing of the full word, that name as long as a railway track that could circle the earth along its equator: I-s-a-b-e-l! Six letters! A fierce struggle for each one and I had not the fortitude to begin the first… nothing!

I had to climb the stairs, climb them happy, radiant and full of the joy that fills the man who has fully passed beyond men. I had, radiant and happy, to flare my nostrils and breathe in, deeper than the depths of all my pleasant memories, the smell of the countryside that the lime flowers wafted over the table and that the table pushed upward through the thick air of my nose. I had to say to my wife's image: 'Our home, our bed, soft light…' And, most importantly: 'Let's go!'

And again, we went out together to walk through the streets and climb into the lift and arrive at our apartment in so exactly, so precisely, the same way that I lay down and asked her to wait for just a few minutes in the next room.

The three little flies again took flight, and one of them went to the toilets to wash its hands. Then I had to relive what had happened a short while ago and for the second time I felt my brain emptying. It emptied out and I sank into absolute inanity.

This emptiness must have been quite complete, for I immediately felt my entire body soften and I was invaded by a languor that was almost beatific. Then, not having an active brain to coordinate it, my body went slack. I was afraid that it would become semi-solid and that it could, with the consistency and relentlessness of a river of lava, spill out in both directions over the sheets towards the edges of the bed.

As a precaution – you never know! – I squeezed my arms against my body and pressed my legs together to maintain their shapes, since they could well disintegrate once they were lacking he who provided their reason for being.

Then the newly acquired impulse to remember was once more channelled within me and, since that impulse was to relive the whole day, I repeated what I had done after the previous emptiness, and I had to say to myself: 'Let's see. The day began with the business of the guillotine.'

And then began the parade of yesterday's events.

It began with a slight hopefulness and a strong fear. The hope was that this time, upon reaching the toilets, my will would be stronger, and I would be able to shout my wife's name and summon her to me, so that I could impart my wisdom and we could seal it within our lives and go on looking at random as before, only now in the light of a brand-new knowledge. The fear was that my remembrance of the day would be stronger than me, that her name would not be articulated, that events would follow the logic of said remembrance and that, as it all happened for the second time in my mind, the third time in total, I would have to go upstairs to drink my lime flower tea, then return home and lie down. Then I would have to remember that in reality I had lain down, that when I lay down I had emptied out, that I had felt my body go slack and that then, in order to seize the great moment, I had begun again at the beginning, I had begun with the guillotine, the guillotine which led to the zoo, which led to lunch, which led to Rubén de Loa's studio, which led to the waiting room and the square, which led to dinner, which led to my family's house, which led to the tavern, which led to the pisser, which led to the hole and the fly that tore time in two and illuminated everything, which... which, no doubt, will make me climb up towards the lime flower tea, doubtless, because this was the truth of how things had happened. The fear was that all of life, from now until my very last moment, would be spent circling through this chain of events, whose last link is the act of wrapping myself in the sheets and remembering the first, which, on being remembered, automatically awakens the second, which... in sum, the third, fourth, fifth, the last, which is to evoke the first, which...

And within this circle, no matter how many times I went around it – and it would be as many times as my life allowed – I would remember that single moment, I would want to retain it, and it would escape me every time, only to return and return.

With that tiny hope, with that crushing fear, my elbows squeezed tight, my legs pressed together, I began.

The guillotine… cuckoo! Yes, all, all.

The lions… the spring-loaded lions. Yes, all, all of it.

The cynocephali… the song. Yes, all, all.

The battle… the elm. Yes, all of it, all. And the deviation of my thoughts as well.

The deviation. Let's see.

At the top of the elm, it was the memory of Belmonte's movement and the wish to talk to my wife about it.

In bed, it was the realization that there in the tree I had remembered something more, I had remembered everything up to the flare of the beautiful Lucrecia's match.

Finally, on realizing this, the true deviation had come. Something had been added that had not occurred there beside the battling creatures: all of Zaragoza, the Zaragoza of those days long past, with my Lucrecia's green mornings.

And now, moving through the circuit for the second time, my Lucrecia's green mornings were augmented.

From an earthy oblivion arose many mooring lines leading back to my life at that time. Not just the hotel, not just Our Lady of the Pillar. The whole city of Zaragoza spread out and, as it spread out, it extended to all the places I had visited in Spain. Everything from my trip. All the people it contained. All that I ascribed of good or bad to those people. That whole time!

But, while that time was pressed into service in my memory and I lived within it like any good man remembering his past in peace, alongside that, the parade of yesterday's events continued its course, making me say to myself that arriving at the match's flame was to get too far away, that I had to return to the skirmish, saying to myself: 'Back in line! Back in line!'

So, the cycle of yesterday continued its course while I freely, or with a relative freedom, palpated and dug my fingertips into all of that solid, stable, hard period that was my trip through Spain, my trip outside of any circle.

And Rubén de Loa went past, went right past. And, from Toledo, I saw him pass. The waiting room happened and Chasuble Square happened and I saw them go by in just the same way.

It was a double life, a parallel simultaneity of the year 1920 and yesterday. Yesterday was an endless circle, my permanent fixation in the process of revolving remembrance; the year 1920 was the flat, vast surface along which I could always run, always slip away from any thought that was too stubborn, from any train of thought that was too insistent.

But this didn't imply a complete detachment from the circle. It was always there. I felt it as though it were positioned above me, emerging from the back of my neck. It was large and reached up to the ceiling of the room. It had something like flat fan blades. As each blade touched my head, it grazed whatever thought of Spain that chance had brought just then to my memory. It grazed it and, as it touched it, snagged it, that memory might well disappear, and in that case – once again I was only on the wheel of yesterday!

In short, although my position was not very firm as I squelched about in that far-off year, and my brain was simultaneously perforated by the blades of the day's events as they turned, in short, Chasuble Square came and went and I confessed to my wife the failure of my observations, laying the blame on the hunger that was gnawing at me.

The Basilica restaurant appeared.

It appeared just as it had in reality, with every one of its stews, and also with the garnish I saw when I remembered it the first time: the ox's head with its two enormous horns. And here, as in the previous case, I saw, with comforting relief, that the parade continued, the procession went on: we were paying the bill, going out into the street and, in spite of all that, the ox remained in my memory!

It remained. The Basilica restaurant did not carry it away, as logic would have had it. No, the head separated and, just like Spain a moment before, that single head spread out into another flat and vast surface that was – even while yesterday's memories filed by – imperceptibly populated with other oxen, with peasants to herd them, with trees motionless in the sun, with hills lulled by birds, with my own self – so many times! ever since I was a child! – ploughing through the years in those fixed pastures, today pinned by the two enormous horns.

Now I was no longer palpating. I dug my nails into those two pieces of my past, calm and stable pieces. Surfaces I had lived and, once lived, left behind, settled and unmoving.

Now I could spiral above them. They did not waver. In their arrested past they could let me alight on them, and as they received me they suggested new surfaces for the future where I could dig in my talons and spit.

Above me the circle turned, from the top of my head leaked the minutiae of the day itself. It turned, immobilizing me in the contemplation of its passing. Now we are going into my family's mansion and our presence provokes in them a frank hilarity.

Go on, go on! The sofa, the thing with legs? Let it come!

I watch, I watch! Nothing more. I find myself, I am my past travels and my pastures that are dotted throughout my life. I still don't have the strength to stop at any part of the circle as it comes. Naturally, I don't have it. Naturally, I have to stand there in the living room and listen, one by one, to Pedro's idiotic utterances. And then?

Ah! Beneath it all, very close by, two sturdy posts are now fixed, toasted by the sun of Spain and by the sun of our country pastures.

Above the suns, the night-time cemetery files past, along with all the possibilities of a man losing his senses, as he might lose them behind a sofa or before a hat.

The Polish man's grave is passing by!

It separates! It falls!

While I say 'No' to Pedro, the grave has fallen and is affixed beside me, elbow to elbow with pastures and travels. Two years the Polish man has lain there. Two years I've been in San Agustín de Tango. Two years since we were parallel, the Polish man and I. He, laid out and worm-eaten; I, standing and careening head first.

Two years. These two years.

The grave – like Lucrecia's green sex, like the ox's horns –

the grave lifted up its headstone and from its hollow, from the Polish man's shrivelled tissue, my life in these past two years emerges, spreads out, is fixed.

There are three posts now. Three robust posts that expand, merge and fuse together, to form three plains that fill my entire past. Now it's my whole past, and all the strength accumulated in it with which to go on living, that oppose the force of this rotating act of remembrance that goes on, goes on and goes on.

Though I spiral and leap freely from Zaragoza to the herds of oxen, from the oxen to the woman who today was my companion as we walked through these streets, from her to my childhood in the fig orchards or to my mute contemplation of Burgos, the cycle I've unleashed goes on. 'Dad, do you think the armies would have stopped when they saw the being from Jupiter?' The cycle continues, the tavern will come, and when it comes, I will steel myself to remember that we ordered lime flower tea and that, when the waiter brought the tea, I had to urinate. And once I remember I had to urinate, I will be forced to remember the five holes and my taking aim in order at one after another without touching the hole in the centre. And at this point, there will be no human strength that can stop the fly from implanting itself in my memory. And when the fly has arrived, the stream of urine will hesitate, causing a hesitation in my very condition as a man passing through time. Glory!

Will I be able to call her? Isabel! Will I be able to?

Let us hope so.

We've entered the Barefoot Tavern. Everything goes on

simultaneously. There is the spinning circle. Here, my freedom.

I must hold as tightly as possible to the three pillars, so that the circle spins loose and escapes like a wheel thrown off at high speed, flying through the air, alone and far away.

There came the memory of the moment when, as time split a second time, I tried to call to her and an 'I' was stifled in my throat. But that time I was alone with the circle, I was inside it and I spun with it. Now, I am outside, almost outside, and the spinning of my head is above me; now, though, three points that mark my past life hold me fast. Plus, to keep me more rooted, I have instinctively moved to flatten myself as much as possible against the mattress, compressing myself with the blankets, to increase in as many ways as possible my freedom from that relentless circular parade of events.

'Isabel!'

I have cried out. I have cried out. My cry has come just as time has stopped passing and has been erased and become single, unpassing and solid.

She has replied: 'Coming!'

But by the time these six letters fully have entered my ears, I am already climbing up the stairs and breathing in the lime flower perfumes, while the three vast, flat plains continue to stretch out towards the horizon, golden in the sun, streaked with mooing, filled with still cities.

My beloved wife takes her time in coming. She goes on with her tasks in the next room. I am already coming home with her; we've already taken the lift, creaking and rising.

For the third time now, I am in bed and my ideas melt into three little flies that take flight.

My wife has finished her tasks. I hear her footsteps coming towards me.

Without ideas, without a brain to bind it, my body slackens. The second time. It will slacken more and liquid will fall to the floor to be stepped in. Even the plains grow shadowy and slip away. Unless I contract my elbows and legs and fill my head, saying to myself: 'Let's see. The day began with the business of the guillotine.'

And the lions will appear. The cynocephali…

As long as she gets here a second or even a hundredth of a second before the third time around!

She keeps walking. Never would I have imagined there was so much space between the two rooms or so much time between two steps.

My body slackens. It spills out over the sheets.

Here it is.

She asks: 'You called?'

Before my body drips away or I start to recall the guillotine, there is still a sliver of time left held up by the three vast plains.

Make the most of them, use them to hold me up!

'My dear wife,' I said to her, 'grab a pen and paper and draw my body.'

'To what end?' she asks me.

'Draw!'

The light of my life draws. My body lies naked on the bed. She transfers it to the paper with a single black line.

'Close the outline!' I say.

'Like this?' she asks, showing me the drawing.

'Like that,' I answer. 'By making a solid shape all the way around, nothing will ever get out.'

It is true. Now my body, drawn there, is confined on all sides. Now it exists once again.

'As far as the day we lived today, my dear, from the guillotine on, we will sum it up and frame it in your drawing of my body. The shape you have made will conserve the day on paper, outside of me. And so now, let's go to sleep.'

'Yes,' she answers, 'let's go to sleep.'

Subscribe

Discover the best of contemporary European literature: subscribe to Peirene Press and receive a world-class novella from us three times a year, direct to your door. The books are sent out six weeks before they are available in bookshops and online.

Your subscription will allow us to plan ahead with confidence and help us to continue to introduce English readers to the joy of new foreign literature for many years to come.

'A class act'
THE GUARDIAN

'Two-hour books to be devoured in a single sitting: literary cinema for those fatigued by film'
TIMES LITERARY SUPPLEMENT

A one year subscription costs £35 (3 books, free p&p for UK)

Please sign up via our online shop at www.peirenepress.com/shop

2021
Peirene STEVNS
TRANSLATION PRIZE

The Peirene Stevns Translation Prize was launched in 2018 to support up-and-coming translators.

Open to all translators without a published novel, this prize looks not only to award great translation but also to offer new ways of entry into the world of professional translation. The winner receives a £3,500 commission to translate a text selected by Peirene Press, the opportunity to spend two months at a retreat in the Pyrenees and a dedicated one-on-one mentorship throughout the translation process.

The Peirene Stevns Prize focuses on a different language each year and is open for submissions from October to January.

With thanks to Martha Stevns, without whom this prize would not be possible.